EUSKAL HERRIA

País Vasco · Basque Country · Pays Basque

sua edizioak

ekar fundazioa

Portuetxe 88, 20018 Donostia
Tel/Fax: 943 219 427
fundazioa@elkar.com
www.elkarfundazioa.org

Epalza 8 - 48007 Bilbao
Tel: 94 416 94 30 Fax: 94 416 69 76
sua@sua-edizioak.com
www.sua-edizioak.com

Text: Hektor Ortega

Translated by: Marta Urcelay

© **Photographs:** Alberto Muro

Other photographs:
Note: The photos are indicated with the page number. When there are two or more photos, we indicate their order on the page (top down and left to right), adding a letter by alphabetic order.
-Bibliothèque nationale de France: 8.
-www.guregipuzkoa.net: 9 (Indalecio Ojanguren), 87 (Car. Vicente Martin, Indalecio Ojanguren, Agencia Keystone and Pascual Marín), 88 (Indalecio Ojanguren), 89 (Indalecio Ojanguren), 94 (Juan San Martin and Jakintza ikastola), 104b (Pascual Marin), 105 (Hondarribiko Udala and Indalecio Ojanguren), 106a (San Martin), 108h (flopez), 109 (Indalecio Ojanguren and Paco Mari Marín)
-Aranzadi Zientzia Elkartea: 34.
-Jose Lopez Jauregi (Estudio José Lopez) 34.
-Elkar artxiboa: 34, 36a, 98c, 108b, 108c and g (Juantxo Egaña), 108i (Eñaut Elorrieta). 140 (Arturo Delgado), 141, 142b,
-Thinkstock: 35 (Martina Berg), 39 (Hemera Tecnologies)
-Nordhi: 46d, 64b.
-Irekia/Gobierno Vasco: 58 (Mikel Arrazola), 60 (Mikel Arrazola), 76, 138 (Mikel Arrazola).
-www.albumsiglo19mendea.net: 82, 83, 84, 103a.
-Archivo de la revista Berton: 85.
-Gure Esku Dago: 91.
-AEK: 99a, 99b, 99e.
-Kezka dantza taldea: 98b, 146.
-Gorka Palazio: 99c
-wwww.aiaraldea.com: 99d
-Nafarroa Oinez 14: 98a
-British Library: 100
-Museo Zumalakarregi: 104a (Gaspar Montes Iturrioz)
-Euskal Kultur Erakundea www.eke.eus: 108a
-www.argia.com: 108d
-Egaroa: 108f
-www.ukberri.net: 110
-www.dantzan.com: 111 (Iñaki Zugasti), 148b, 148c, 149a
-TaraO: 124b
-Gorobel: 125b
-Celso Flores: 125a
-Quincena Musical: 142a
-Donostia Kultura: 143 (Gorka Bravo).
-Asier Solana Bermejo: 147.
-Ertzetik: 151b (Asier Gogortza).

Cover photograph: Haizearen orrazia (the Wind Comb). Donostia (Alberto Muro)

Design: Aurkene Etxebarria

Print: Leitzaran Grafikak

ISBN: 978-84-8216-558-5

Legal deposit: SS 1393-2014

2014

This book is based on 'Euskal Herria. A country', published by Sua in 1998, and on the text in the book, written by Alex Ugalde Zubiri.

INDEX

PROLOGUE

Euskal Herria cannot be summed up in a few words. The country may be small, but the Basque people are too great to fit into a paragraph. Euskal Herria has a rich, ancestral past, with deep roots, an ancient culture and a language that is lost in the mists of time. It is a compendium of stunning landscapes, from the rough and stormy blue of the ocean to the rugged peaks that march towards the Pyrenees. From the earthy pigments of the wine-growing plains to the cool, green orchards. Euskal Herria exudes art in old buildings on lonely estates and in ancestral towns; and also in stunning buildings made of glass, titanium or twisted steel. The valleys resound with the echo of verses sung over hundreds of years, the chords of dances handed down from one generation to the next, and the revelry of our festivities. Above all, Euskal Herria is a people and a sentiment. Gradually, Basque men and women have made this country what it is. We imbue it with personality and make it greater every step of the way.

The future of the language is uncertain. We could blame our changing times, where everything is fleeting, or the ills of the 21st century, where uniformity threatens to obliterate identities and singularities. Yes, it would be easy to give modern times such power, but we must not allow it. To look into the future is to be aware of the past, and the Basques are in a good position to do that: we know who we are and where we come from. We seek our place in the world with modest self-confidence.

This book shares the values of the Elkar Foundation and, therefore, it is an investment in the future. A future that the Foundation supports by promoting and developing the Basque language and culture. A future that is present in the eagerness not only to equal our past, but to surpass it. It is a fond, heart-felt tour of Euskal Herria. We seek to make the Basques known to those who know nothing about us, but the book also targets those who live in the Basque Country, have a deep sense of belonging and are committed to a common future. This book is dedicated to you, with all the enthusiasm in the world.

JOXEMARI SORS
ELKAR FOUNDATION

A profusion of NAMES for a country that doesn't exist

Let's start with a confession. The Basque Country has some disconcerting aspects that can be rather baffling when first encountered. An example would be the number of names it is known by, like a spy with many aliases. This is not very surprising. After all, we are talking about a country that does not exist; at least, not officially. You won't find it on an ordinary political map and even less in the UN General Assembly. The name used to refer to it depends on the different ways in which people, organisations and institutions view the country. The meanings of the names and the manner in which they are used have also evolved over time. Moreover, the same name may refer to the entire country or only a part of it, adding to the confusion. It is a muddle that is hard to untangle.

Nonetheless, it does not necessarily have to be confusing. To native speakers of Basque, the name is not particularly complicated. In their language, the Basque people refer mainly to only one name: *Euskal Herria*, the people of Euskera, as their language is known in Basque. They call themselves the *euskaldunak*, or those who speak Basque. It is a very loose way of considering what it means to belong to a people: to them, knowing the language is enough.

Such extreme simplicity is in sharp contrast with the long list of names that have been used in other languages, even by the Basque themselves: the Basque Country, Navarre-Basque Country, Euskadi, Euskaria, Vascongadas, Navarre; the Spanish Basque Country and French Basque Country; Peninsular Euskadi and Continental Euskadi; the Northern Basque Country (Iparralde) and Southern Basque Country (Hegoalde); Pays Basque, and so forth. There are also other names that now seem absurd, such as Cantabria, which was commonplace. Not so long ago, it was believed that the Romans never even occupied the country. The notion that the ancient Cantabrian people were the forebears of the Basques was fiercely defended at the turn of the nineteenth century.

Map included in a codex manuscript in Saint-Sever (Landes, France), written c.1060. It places Wasconia near the bottom, above the Pyrenees. It is the first time that Euskal Herria appears on a known map.

A political act in the Meeting House in Gernika, in the early 20th century. The old oak tree has been a symbol of Basque freedoms for centuries.

Curiously enough, the most popular name in the twentieth century, Euskadi or Euzkadi, is a neologism created by Sabino Arana, the founder of Basque nationalism, in 1899. A people with so many names had to invent another name to be able to recognise themselves. The need existed, for even the term *vasco* (Basque), applied to the country as a whole, only harked back to the nineteenth century. Before the nineteenth century, the Land of the Basques comprised the territories of Labourd (Lapurdi), Soule (Zuberoa) and, above all, Lower Navarre (Nafarroa Beherea). Therefore, only the natives of those provinces were Basque. Before the term 'Basque' became widespread, which occurred in French first (*basque*), several terms had been used in Spanish to

País Vasco, Vasconia, País Vasco-Navarro,
Euskadi, Euskaria, Vascongadas, Navarra,
País Vasco-Español y País Vasco-Francés,
Euskadi Peninsular y Euskadi Continental,
Euskadi Norte y Euskadi Sur,
Iparralde y Hegoalde, Pays Basque...•

Euskal Herria

designate the natives of the country as a whole: *vizcaíno*, *navarro*, and *vascongado* (the people of Biscay, Navarre and the Basque Country, respectively). San Francisco Javier, a nineteenth century saint from Navarre, referred to his language, Basque, as the "language of the people of Biscay".

Contrary to the variety of names used throughout history to designate the country and its people, the term *Euskal Herria* was already being used in the dawn of Basque literature. Álava-born Joan Pérez de Lazarraga included it several times in his mid-nineteenth century chivalric verses, as in "*...zegaiti dozun Euskel Erria ainbat bentajaz dotadu...*". Shortly after, at the other end of the country, Labourd-born Joanes Leizarraga also used the term in his translation of the New Testament (1571): "*...ukanen duela sartze eta avamendu Heuskalherrian*". In the following century, it was Pedro Agerre *Axular*, from Navarre, who explained in his classical work *Gero* (1643) that the Basque language was spoken in Euskal Herria, with local variations: "*Ceren anhitz moldez eta differentqui minçatcen baitira eufcal herrian. Naffarroa garayan, Naffarroa beherean, Çuberoan, Lappurdin, Bizcayan, Guipuzcoan, Alaba-herrian, eta bertce anhitz leccutan (...)*". In his quote he listed the territories encompassed by the term for the first time: Upper Navarre, Lower Navarre, Soule (Zuberoa), Labourd (Lapurdi), Biscay, Guipúzcoa and Álava. He added that Euskera (the Basque language) was also spoken in other places, probably in reference to the adjacent Béarnese regions, which were Basque-speaking until recently.

Five centuries later, the term Euskal Herria bears witness to the existence of a tangible and cultural reality born of thousands of years of coexistence that goes beyond borders, religions, wars and political divisions. It is what Eusko Ikaskuntza, the Basque Studies Society, defines as "a European cultural space or region located on either side of the Pyrenees that comprises territories that are in Spain and France. Therefore, Euskal Herria or the land of the Basques is the space where the Basque culture is strongly manifested". Euskaltzaindia, the Academy of the Basque Language, has also pointed out how appropriate the name Euskal Herria is "to refer to the seven territories or provinces without referring to a specific administrative body". Moreover, after a reminder of the term's widespread use from the nineteenth century onwards, even in Spanish and by every political family, the Academy emphasises that "a secular tradition deserves respect and no one has the right to change it at their whim".

In this guide, we adhere to tradition and employ the term Euskal Herria to refer to the Basque country as a whole.

Esssential GUIDE to find your way in a pocket-size country

Geographic position

It isn't easy to find Euskal Herria on modern maps. You'll get no hits when you write its name to search for it on Google maps. To find such a mysterious country, you must look for Europe and then locate the point where Spain and France touch each other in the Bay of Biscay.

For advanced surfers, these are its coordinates: latitudes 43º 32' 30" and 41º- 54' 34" North and longitudes 0º 43' 22" and 3º 20' 30" West. When the numbers are entered on the map, the keen observer will notice that these are average European latitudes subject to Atlantic, continental and Mediterranean influences. Hence the environmental and climatic diversity of the Basque Country.

Borders

Divided between Spain and France, Euskal Herria has no official frontier or sign to indicate its borders. It is bounded to the northeast with Béarn (in the French department of Pyrénées-Atlantiques); to the north with the Landes department, with which it shares the last section of the river Adour (Aturri, in the Basque language); to the northwest with the Bay

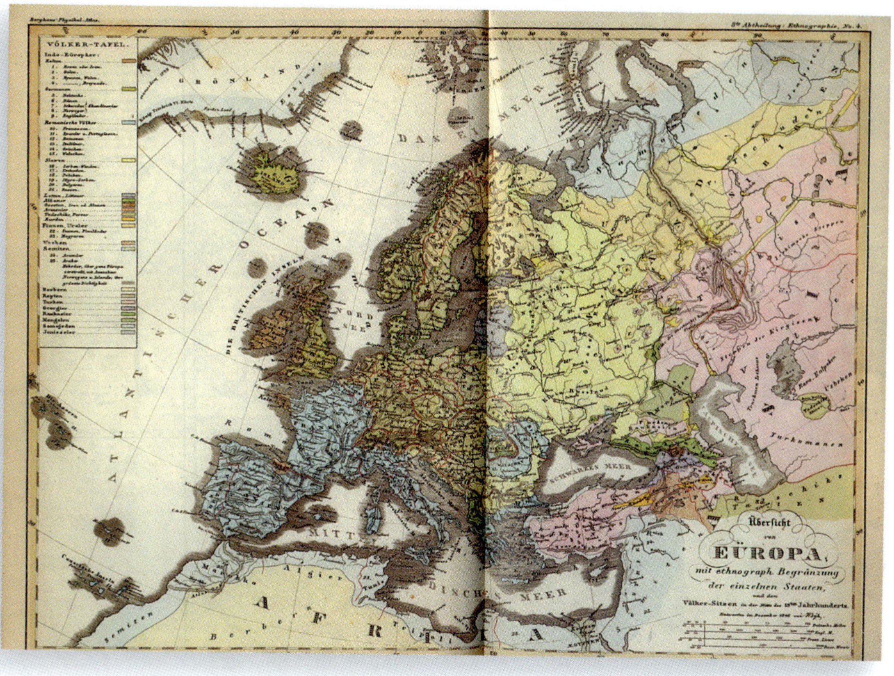

Übersicht von Europa, mit ethnograph. Begränzung der eizelnen Staaten, und den Völker-Sitzen in der Mitte des 19ten Jahrhunderts. Entwarfen in December 1846 von Wogh. An overview of Europe with the ethnographic outline of the states and location of different peoples in the mid-19th century. Drawn by Wolg in December 1846. A German map that appears in Dr Heinrich Berghaus' Physikalisher Atlas, one of the crown jewels of German cartography, edited by Justus Perthes in 1848 and reissued by the Eichborn publishing house in Frankfort in 2004. *Vasken*, highlighted in colour, includes the seven Basque territories, from Bayonne to the line of the river Ebro.

Seven territories

There are seven historical territories in Euskal Herria: Lapurdi (Labourd, in French; Labort in Spanish), whose capital is Baiona-Bayonne; Nafarroa Beherea (Basse Navarre/Lower Navarre), whose capital is Donibane Garazi-Saint Jean Pied de Port; Zuberoa (Soule/Sola), whose capital is Maule-Mauleón; Araba (Álava), whose capital is Vitoria-Gasteiz; Bizkaia (frequently called Biscay in English), whose capital is Bilbo-Bilbao; Gipuzkoa, whose capital is Donostia-San Sebastián; and Nafarroa (Navarre/Navarra), whose capital is Iruñea-Pamplona.

Seven governments

Euskal Herria is a land that straddles two States (France and Spain). In Spain, three provinces (Araba, Bizkaia and Gipuzkoa) make up the Basque Autonomous Region or Euskadi, while Nafarroa is a separate autonomous region. The three northern provinces (Labourd/Lapurdi, Lower Navarre/Nafarroa Beherea and Soule/Zuberoa are in the French Department of Pyrénées-Atlantiques and the region of Aquitaine. Moreover, the Villaverde de Trucíos enclave belongs to the autonomous region of Cantabria and the Trebiño enclave belongs to the autonomous region of Castilla-León.

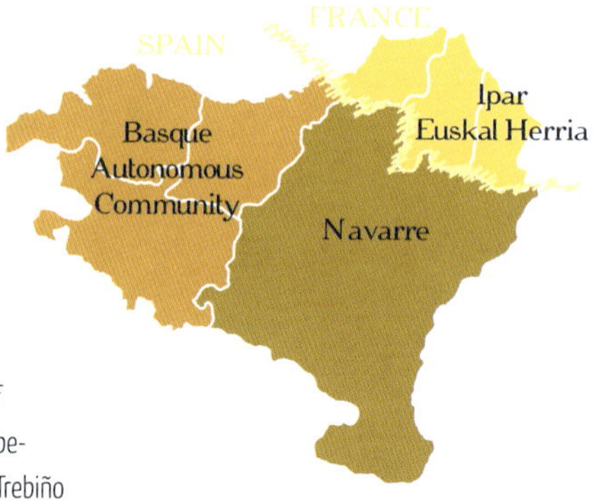

in data

TOTAL AREA	20.960 km²
Nafarroa	10.421 km² (50.48%)
Araba	3.312 km² (14.76%)
Bizkaia	2.236 km² (10.73%)
Gipuzkoa	1.997 km² (9.62%)
N. Beherea	1.336 km² (6.46%)
Lapurdi	857 km² (4.14%)
Zuberoa	789 km² (3.8%)

Coats of arms to the two territories

Nafarroa

Araba

Bizkaia

Gipuzkoa

Lapurdi

Nafarroa Beherea

Zuberoa

Ikurriña Flag

of Biscay (Atlantic Ocean); to the west with the Spanish autonomous communities of Cantabria and Castilla-León (province of Burgos); to the south with the autonomous community of La Rioja, separated from it by the Ebro River for many kilometres; and to the east and southeast with the autonomous community of Aragón (provinces of Saragossa/Zaragoza and Huesca).

Seven territories, many divisions

In Euskara, *zazpi* means 'seven' and also, in some cases, 'many'. The historical territories of Euskal Herria are not many, but seven: Lapurdi (or Labourd, in French), whose capital is Baiona-Bayonne; Nafarroa Beherea (Lower Navarre), whose capital is Donibane Garazi-Saint Jean Pied de Port; Zuberoa (Soule), whose capital is Maule-Mauleón; Araba (Álava), whose capital is Vitoria-Gasteiz; Bizkaia (frequently called Biscay in English), whose capital is Bilbo-Bilbao; Gipuzkoa, whose capital is Donostia-San Sebastián; y Nafarroa (Navarre), whose capital is Iruñea-Pamplona.

Divided between Spain and France, the seven territories are further divided into many administrative areas. Continental Euskal Herria (or North, Ipar Euskal Herria) comprises Labourd, Lower Navarre and Soule. The three territories belong to France. In 1790 they were integrated (together with Béarn) in the department of the Lower Pyrenees (now the department of Pyrénées-Atlantiques), whose main town is Pau. In turn, the department is within the region of Aquitaine. There are two subdivisions of the department (those of Baiona and Oloron) that do not respect the reality of the country either. Labourd, Lower Navarre and a small part of Zuberoa are grouped into one department; and the rest of Zuberoa and Béarn in the other. Peninsular Euskal Herria (or South, Hego Euskal Herria) comprises Araba, Bizkaia, Gipuzkoa and Navarre. Administratively, the four territories belong to Spain, although currently they are divided into two autonomous communities: the Basque autonomous community, or Euskadi (the provinces of Araba, Bizkaia and Gipuzkoa), whose capital is Vitoria-Gasteiz; and the autonomous community of Navarre, whose capital is Iruñea-Pamplona.

A pocket-size country

Euskal Herria covers an area of 20,960 km^2. A small country, without doubt. From a hypothetical geographical centre in the heart of the Andia mountains, we could hardly walk more than 150 km in any direction without leaving the country. Navarre is more extensive; with 10,421 km^2, it occupies 50.48% of the total area. The other provinces are much more modest in size: Araba 3,312 km^2 (14.76% of the total), Bizkaia 2,236 km^2 (10.73%), Gipuzkoa 1,997 km^2 (9.62%) and Lower Navarre 1,336 km^2 (6.46%). Two small territories end the list: Labourd, with 857 km^2 (4.14%) and Soule, with 789 km^2 (3.8%). We should point out that we have added the 279 km^2 of the county of Trebiñu (279 km^2) to Araba, although Trebiñu is currently under the administration of Castilla-León; and the 19.64 km^2 of Villaverde de Trucíos, which officially belongs to Cantabria, have been added to Bizkaia.

Zazpiak zazpi. Seven governments

Despite its small size, Euskal Herria boasts quite a number of governments. Apart from the governments of the two countries spanned by Euskal Herria (France and Spain), there are also the Basque government, the government of Navarre and the Regional Council of Aquitaine. To this list we must add the governments of the Spanish autonomous communities of Cantabria and Castilla-León, whose administrations govern the two abovementioned enclaves: Villaverde de Trucíos and Trebiñu. That makes seven governments in all; quite a few for so small a country.

Elementary CARTOGRAPHY

A winding country

Seen from the air, Euskal Herria could be described as a broad limestone backbone besieged by two extensive plains. An imposing mountain range traverses the country from east to west, losing majesty and height as it approaches the sea. It is the Pyrenees mountain range, which continues in Bizkaia, Gipuzkoa and Araba in the form of a sea of smaller mountains surrounded by valleys. To the north, the sinuous landscape ends abruptly when it encounters the extensive plains of Aquitaine. To the south, the broad Ebro Valley also softens the topography, although less successfully.

The Pyrenees lose altitude as they advance towards the west, penetrating Euskal Herria along the Three Kings Plateau-Hiru Erregeen Mahaia, the highest point in the country, with an altitude of 2,428 metres. The first (or last, depending on whether you are looking from the east or the west) two-thousand metre peak, the Orhi, lies twenty kilometres further on. After that landmark, the Pyrenees drop to altitudes of 1,500 metres (the peaks of Abodi, Urkulu and Lindus) and even lower among the valleys of Baigorri, Baztan and Xareta (Auza, Iparla and Artzamendi) until they arrive at their last great landmark, Mount Larrun, which overlooks the coast of Lapurdi from a modest height of 900 metres.

On the northern slopes, the Arbaila and Harsudurra massifs become detached from the Pyrenees, making the boundary between Soule and Lower Navarre seem more important. The boundary between the latter and Labourd also boasts a group of mountains, but they are less spectacular than their neighbours. Apart from these, there are little more than hills as you move north and reach the river Aturri-Adour.

A group of mountains to the west seem to prolong the Pyrenees, but at lower elevations of 1,000 to 1,500 metres. From Baztan, passing by

The Errezil valley viewed from the top of the Ernio mountain (Gipuzkoa)

The boulders of Axkorrigan rise proudly above the Orozko valley (Bizkaia)

Saioa and Belate, the mountain chain that acts as a dividing watershed between the Mediterranean Sea and the Atlantic Ocean crosses the entire country westward, past the Aralar, Aratz-Aizkorri, Anboto-Urkiola and Gorbeia ranges, and the Gorobel-Salvada massif, until it enters Burgos.

Another pre-Pyrenean barrier runs through Navarre and Araba in the same direction. The mountains of Leire, Izko, Alaitz, Erreniega/El Perdón, Andia, Urbasa, Entzia, Iturrieta, Kodes, Lokiz, Montes de Vitoria, Izki and Toloño drop to the southwest until they come to the river Ebro.

The coastline of Bizkaia and Gipuzkoa is dotted with low mountains that are rarely attain 1,000 metres above sea level (Aiako Harria, Oiz, Ganekogorta). Nonetheless, they occupy almost the entire territory, making the surrounding valleys very narrow, with few flat spaces, surrounded by a swarm of minor vantage points overlooking the Bay of Biscay.

Valleys are another feature of the landscape. Valleys that are mostly deep and narrow, with a south-north orientation on the coast of Bizkaia and Gipuzkoa, with the exception of the Ibaizabal and Butroe river basins. Valleys that follow the rivers Barbadún, Oka, Lea, Artibai, Deba, Urola, Oria and Urumea. In Ipar Euskal Herria, they follow the main rivers, such as the Uhaitzandia (Saison), which provides the essential structure of Zuberoa, Errobi (Nive) and Biduze (Bidouze), making broader spaces. There are still narrow sections in the heads of the valleys, however, as in Santa Grazi and Aldude. Something similar occurs in Baztan with the river Bidasoa.

On the Mediterranean coast, on the other hand, the Pyrenean valleys are oriented from north to south, forming spaces flanked by tall mountains interspersed by narrow passes known as *foces* or *ateak*. Erronkaribar/Roncal, Zaraitzu/Salazar and Artzibar/Arce boast these characteristics. When they open out southwards, the valleys become wider and the massifs smaller. The Plains of Alava, Sakana, the basins of Iruñea/Pamplona, Agoitz and Irunberri/Lumbier form a passage that traverses the centre of the country. The landscape softens and becomes less wrinkled as it extends southward and penetrates the depression formed by the river Ebro.

A short but intensive coast

The Basque coast is 225 km long from Covaron (Bizkaia) to the mouth of the river Aturri-Adour in Baiona. Except for the Baiona-Biarritz section, consisting of ten straight kilometres of sand, the rest faces the waves in the Bay of Biscay with brave defiance. It is not by accident that this is a high coastline, defended by formidable cliffs and a dozen uninhabitable islands, where the only apertures are the inlets and estuaries. Ports have been built in every nook and cranny that can afford protection for vessels, however small the space may be.

All through the twentieth century, human pressure – first industrial and later urban – disfigured and polluted the country's main estuaries and urbanised its beaches. Nonetheless, the Basque Country still preserves many kilometres of pristine coastline and some of the most spoiled sections have been partially recovered. In fact, the coast boasts some of the country's main attractions: magic places such as San Juan de Gaztelugatxe, picturesque fishing ports such as the one in Zokoa; geological landmarks such as the *flysh* in Deba and Zumaia; and nature areas such as the Urdaibai Biosphere Reserve.

The temperature of the sea along the Basque coast varies between 11 ºC-13 ºC in winter and 21 ºC-22 ºC in summer. These are temperate waters, due to the influence of the Golf Stream, a warm Atlantic ocean current that originates in

The rocky cove
of Natxitua (Bizkaia)

the Gulf of Mexico. The temperature of the sea contributes to the mild climate along the Basque coastline, which is warmer than normal for its latitude, with few variations.

This rocky coast has witnessed the passage of Roman galleys – the *via maris* navigated by traders along most of Europe's Atlantic coast – and Viking *drakkars*. Some scholars suspect that what the Basques learned from the Vikings encouraged them to venture across the ocean in the Late Middle Ages. Since then, they have captured whales on the Basque coast and cod in Newfoundland; traded with Flanders, the Indies and the Philippines; and in the early twenty-first century they continue to catch tuna in the seas of Africa, Asia and Oceania. Here, along the Basque coast, a dozen modern lighthouses search the horizon for seamen to guide back home.

San Juan de Gaztelugatxe (Bizkaia), an ancient islet artificially joined to the mainland by a narrow passage. Below, the *flysch* in Zumaia (Gipuzkoa), a geological treasure of the Basque cliffs.

Source of the river Larraun, in the Larraun valley (Navarre). These waters will make the long journey to the Mediterranean Sea.

Rivers between two seas

On the Basque coast, logically, only the rivers of the Atlantic Basin flow into the sea. However, the country's largest rivers in terms of volume flow into the river Ebro and travel more than 500 km, to Tortosa. The Atlantic rivers are short, turbulent and have a constant flow. The most important ones make up the Ibaizabal basin (the rivers Cadagua, Nervión and Ibaizabal); the four axes of Gipuzkoa (the Deba, Urola, Oria and Urumea), and the river Urdazuri-Nivelle, which flows into the lovely bay of Donibane Lohizune-San Juan de Luz. The main rivers of this basin, however, for their volume, catchment and direction, are the aforementioned Ibaizabal, the Bidasoa and the tributaries of the river Aturri-Adour (the Uhaitzandi-Saison, Biduze-Bidouze and Errobi-Nive). The river Aturri is 335 km long and does not enter Basque territory until it comes to Bidaxune/Bidache, less than 20 km from Baiona.

All the torrents and rivers that flow south end by joining the river Ebro, which carries them to the Mediterranean. We are referring to the longest rivers with the most volume, although they have a lower level of water in summer. The rivers soon meander gently through the plains and valley floors until they join the main river. From Sobrón, where the Ebro enters Araba, until Cortes, the town where it leaves Navarre, the great Basque river, as the Ebro was once known, travels 200 km, mostly along the country's border. Its main tributaries are the river Arga, which traverses the centre of Navarre from north to south along 161 km; and the river Aragón, which catches the Pyrenean waters of Ezka and

The river Nervión plunges 200 metres as soon as it emerges from the Santiago mountain, in Delika (Araba).

Irati before becoming narrower in Galipentzu to circle the desert of Bardenas. "*Arga and Aragón hacen al Ebro varón*" (The Arga and the Aragón make the Ebro mighty), say the lyrics of the Spanish song and dance known as a *jota*. The song forgets other relevant tributaries, such as the river Ega, which receives most of the water from Tierra Estella; and the rivers that flow through Alava, which are the Baias, and, above all, the Zadorra, the great river that runs through the plains of La Llanada. These are the rivers of the Ebro basin that have been dammed to ensure a water supply for the big cities and, in some cases, to irrigate crops. The Sobrón, Uribarri-Ganboa and the Urrunaga, in Araba; and the Esa, Allotz, Eugi and Itoiz, in Navarre, are small blue islands in the heart of the country.

The Basque rivers flow through some singular landscapes. Such is the case of the Salto del Nervión waterfall, where the river Nervión, still a stream, plunges over a 220 metres (721ft) precipice. It is the highest waterfall in Spain. Another unique feature is the underground streams that originate in the karstic massif of Larra, in Navarre. The stream known as San Martin has carved out the La Verna cavern, in Santa Grazi (in Zuberoa). It is an underground space that is 150 metres in height at the centre, with a floor area of 250 x 200 metres. The cave is so large that it boasts an 80 metre waterfall inside it. It is truly a unique place.

Green, white and... reddish

He probably wasn't thinking of it when he designed the Basque flag, but the three colours that Sabino Arana chose for Euskal Herria's flag are a perfect reflection of the country's three climates. As it does everywhere, the climate depends on physical factors, including latitude, prevailing winds, ocean currents. On the strength of those criteria alone, Euskal Herria could be described as green, with an Atlantic climate; white, owing to its subalpine climate; and ochre or reddish, in the areas with a Mediterranean-continental climate. In this little country you only have to travel a few kilometres to go from an alpine to a desert scenario, including the transition areas between the two extremes.

White Euskal Herria

The mountain or subalpine climate affects the Pyrenean part of Euskal Herria, which lies south of Lower Navarre and Zuberoa, and northeast of Navarre. It is a small area, only a few hundred square kilometres situated at 1,500 m to 2,450 m above sea level. This means that the year round average temperatures are low and particularly cold in winter, when they often drop below freezing. The harsh climate is not limited to the cold, however. Thunder storms, icy mists and fierce winds lash a land that affords no shelter of any sort. The abundant rainfalls with an average annual precipitation of 1,500 mm are normally in the form of snow for seven months of the year, from October to April. The highest areas are covered in snow throughout most of that period, creating a picturesque white backdrop to the mountain scenery.

Green Euskal Herria

The ocean or Atlantic climate extends over the northern half of Euskal Herria: all of Bizkaia, Gipuzkoa and Lapurdi; north of Araba; northwest of Navarre; and the centre and north of Lower Navarre and Zuberoa. It is a textbook example of a humid temperate climate. It is temperate on account of the cool summers (with an average temperature of 18 ºC to 21 ºC) and mild winters (an average 7 ºC to 8 ºC) The annual mean temperature is around 12 ºC, with no marked fluctuations. It is humid on account of the Atlantic low pressure system that discharges part of its load here. That is why it rains all year round (1,000 to 1,500 mm annually), even in summer. The rainiest seasons, however, are spring and autumn. In winter it may snow occasionally, but it only settles for any length of time on the highest peaks. The temperatures grow progressively milder as you approach the sea. This area of Euskal Herria is perennially green.

Ochre Euskal Herria

The Mediterranean climate extends along southern Araba to central and southern Navarre. This is the scenario of sharp contrasts, warm summers (an average 22 ºC in summer) and cold winters, where the temperatures may vary more than 15 ºC. The rainfall is less regular and abundant, with less than 1,000 mm and in some places, such as Las Bardenas, even less than 500 mm. The masses of cold air from the ocean have already discharged most of their load on the coastal mountain ranges by the time they arrive in this area. That is why there are more sunny days throughout the year as you move further south. Naturally, the clear skies can also be contradictory: the frost can be severe and very detrimental for this thriving agricultural region. It is a good idea to seek shelter from the *cierzo*, a cold, dry wind that freezes even the hardiest souls in winter.

Vivid contrast between the dark green foliage surrounding the Harpea cave, in the Irati forest, the red clay of the Bardenas, and the white, snow-clad mountains.

paisaiak, paisajes, paysage
landscapes

The old mines have filled with water, turning them into beautiful lakes. Zugaztieta/La Arboleda. BIZKAIA.

The Holtzarte footbridge crosses a deep ravine in a stunning landscape. Larrañe. ZUBEROA.

A unique view of Valderejo in spring. ARABA.

paisaiak, paisajes, paysage

landscapes

Detail of the Pozalagua cave. Karrantza. BIZKAIA.

Baltzola cave, another magic spot. Dima. BIZKAIA.

Larrunarri or Txindoki, always beautiful. GIPUZKOA.

A country of FORESTS and DESERTS

The Irati forest covers the northern slope of the Abodi mountains (Navarre).

Endless forests and modest clumps of plants, vast meadows, plantations of exotic trees and even semi-arid steppes can be found in Euskal Herria. As it occurs in many other places, the vegetation we find today in our small country is the result of environmental factors (climate, orography, type of soil and so forth) and the prolonged presence of humans, who have transformed the landscape decisively since the Neolithic Period. Hardly any of the original vegetation is left, if it ever existed, for Nature is always changing its appearance as the environmental conditions change and new species emerge. Such is the case of the beech trees, which seem to have been here always, and yet they are a newly arrived species compared to some varieties of oak. According to the experts, beeches have only grown on our mountains for the past six thousand years. As a result of natural alterations and human interference, the Basque topography boasts landscapes with a wide range of vegetation. Even the plants on each side of a single mountain may vary, depending on whether they face north or south. In common with other cultures, the Basque people have venerated some species of trees, such as beeches and hawthorns. They have commended themselves to their protection, as in the case of laurel trees

and thistles, or turned them into a symbol of their freedoms (the Tree of Gernika). It was mandatory in the past to apologise to a tree before felling it: *Guk botako zaitugu eta barkatu iguzu* (Please forgive us, for we are going to fell you).

The last of the Atlantic forests

There was a time when the coastal regions of the country were covered in extensive Atlantic forests. In those days, three large tree species predominated over the region: oaks, beeches and chestnuts. Diseases and the human impact have cut back and nearly wiped out the oak and chestnut forests in many areas. These two species prefer to grow at medium-low altitudes and therefore they give way to a preponderance of beech woods at 500 metres above sea level. The latter made up the most extensive type of forest in the country. The Atlantic forests are enriched with species such as ash trees, elms, lime trees, holly trees, yews, birches (with their attractive white bark), alders and maples (which lend autumn a touch of elegance). Some species make up forests of considerable size, whereas others are stand alone in the midst of glades.

Forests of an assortment of species are not rare, particularly in forests that grow along the banks of the rivers that flow into the Bay of Biscay. Ferns are frequent on the fringes of the Atlantic forests, in the clearings, and on the bare mountain slopes, as well as hazel trees, yellow-flowered broom, common hawthorns, strawberry trees and thorny *rosaceae*, such as blackthorns. Heather and gorse grow where the forests have receded. Scrub oak forests grow in some spots along coasts of Bizkaia and Gipuzkoa, although the species is actually Mediterranean. Combined with other species, such as strawberry trees, laurels and climbing bushes, they make up the Cantabrian scrub oak woods, a true relic of warmer periods. Clover, dandelions, colourful primulaceae,

Extensive beech woods in the Urbasa mountains.

dwarf thistles (known as *eguzkilore* or the sun flower) and orchids are the most common flowers found on the Atlantic slopes. Extensive pastures occupy the highest areas. The native vegetation in Bizkaia, Gipuzkoa, parts of northwestern Navarre and northern Araba

A farmhouse in the shade of the Untzillatx mountain (Bizkaia). Pine trees, young beech trees and meadows.

An autumn landscape in the Baztan valley (Navarre). The entire forest is ablaze with colour.

has been replaced with fast-growing conifers (insignis pines, larches and cypress trees) and Australian eucalyptus. The new species have altered the landscape substantially, to the point of making it unrecognisable in some of the coastal regions of Bizkaia.

Forests between two worlds

Straddling the Atlantic and Mediterranean regions, a transition forest predominates in the middle section of Euskal Herria. If we may say so, it combines the best of both worlds. The transition area is populated by most of the species that are present in the Atlantic forests, although that depends on which way the slopes are facing. Thus, the Atlantic trees prefer the north slopes that receive the moist winds from the ocean, and

the Mediterranean varieties, such as gall oaks, downy oaks and Pyrenean oaks grow on all the other slopes. The resulting contrast in landscape and biodiversity is dramatic.

The shrub stratum comprises juniper trees and hawthorns. Beech woods grow at the highest altitudes and forests of Scots pine in western Araba and northeastern Navarre. Transition vegetation grows in the Llanada Alavesa and is frequent in the Urbasa and Andia mountains (Navarre). The forests on the northern slopes of the Toloño mountains (Araba) mark the southern boundary of beech trees in the Basque Country.

The most southerly and largest (50 hectares) oak forest (common oak) is preserved in nearby Urizaharra-Peñacerrada (southern Araba).

A regal, arid steppe covers a large part of the Bardenas in La Ribera, in Navarre. Below, the domain of black pines, rocks and snow in the karst, in Larra (Navarre).

Mediterranean Aleppo pines

Mediterranean forests thrive in the south of Euskal Herria, where the dry climate is hot in summer and cold in winter. This is the home to the holm oak, gall oak and the classical Mediterranean Aleppo pines. Shrubs predominate near the timber line, mainly junipers, kermes oaks (a small oak barely two metres tall that grows in thick clumps), boxwood, savin juniper, rosemary, honeysuckle and heather. The festival of aromas, flavours and colours is completed with the aromatic species, including thyme, lavender, broom, blackthorns and violets, as well as poppies, orchids, thistles, bearberries and strawberry trees. The dry climate and farming since Roman times are the reasons for the lack of extensive forests in this area. They say that the Rioja Alavesa was covered by an extensive forest of Aleppo pines before humans started to make room for grapevines. Of the luxuriant forests of the past only a few stands are left, but a tour of the woods in the valley of Lana, Kanpezu and the Uxue mountains give an idea of what they were like.

Arid steppe

Southern Navarre boasts semidesert areas with steppe-like vegetation like the extensive Las Bárdenas region where bleak clay landscapes are interspersed with dry scrublands and a few pi-

ne woods. Curiously, these areas are bordered by some of the country's mightiest rivers, such as the Aragón and Ebro, where spectacular riparian forests of black and silver poplars grow. For centuries the grazing land of Las Bárdenas provided sustenance for livestock from the Pyrenean valleys of Navarre in autumn and winter.

Beech trees in the Entzia mountains (Araba)

Cold steppe

Apart from the arid steppe, Euskal Herria also boasts a cold steppe on the summits of the highest mountains, at 1,500 metres above sea level. This is where the forests have given way to grazing land, and to snow for most of the year. Black pines, which can live for up to 600 years, and fir trees grow in full splendour in northeastern Navarre, where the Pyrenees are at their highest. Instead of forming forests, these species stand in groups of individual trees on the rock subalpine steppe. In the karst in Larra, in the northwestern tip of Navarre, at an altitude of more than 2,000 metres in extreme weather conditions, the black pine colonises the rocky ledges by growing on a shrub stratum composed of rhododendrons, common junipers, savin junipers and native plants. The group of hardy survivors makes up a forest steppe that is considered by experts to be a unique landscape in the Pyrenees.

The highlands

The vegetation that grows on the lower mountain ranges is characteristic of the highlands and an Atlantic climate. Beech woods, firs, Scots pines, bearberries and birches alternate with alpine meadows at successive altitudes, depending on the type of soil, climate and altitude. Here we should also include the most important forest in the country, the Irati forest, which covers an extensive area of around 20,000 hectares that spans Zuberoa, Lower Navarre (the canton of Garazi) and the valleys of Aezkoa and Zaraitzu/Salazar in northern Navarre. Here beeches predominate, divided between the Atlantic beech woods of the Aezkoa area and the birch and fir forests of the Zaraitzu/Salazar area.

Vegetation on the edge of the cliff facing the San Anton de Getaria mountain (Gipuzkoa).

Sea cliff flowers

Despite the enormous urban and industrial pressure it has endured in many places, the Basque coast still preserves special plant communities that vary according to their habitat: cliffs, beaches, sandy dunes and estuaries. Small bushes and plants such as maidenhair ferns, coastal ferns, French tamarisks and *Armeria euscadiensis*, a plant with pink flowers that is native to this coast, grow on the cliffs. Heather and gorse are common on the top of the sea cliffs, as well as open areas of heathland and clumps of Atlantic forest and Cantabrian oak groves. Plants that are resistant to drought, high salinity, and exposure to the sun, wind and shifting sands grow on the edges of the beaches and dunes. Trees planted by humans have replaced the native vegetation in some dune areas, as in the case of the maritime pines on the coast of Labourd. Rushes and reeds grow in the estuaries and marshes, where they are subject to inflows of fresh water and seawater mixed by the tides. They form extensive 'underwater prairies' in the places where they are covered by the high tides.

Exposed to the sea

We cannot conclude this section on plant life without mentioning the sea, the natural habitat of algae and lichens. Aquatic plants display a pleasant variety of shapes and colours: green algae (chlorophytes) are the most common; brown algae (phaeophyta) like cold water; and red algae (rhodophyta) prefer warmer, shallower environments. At some points along the coastline it has been customary to collect algae from the beaches and rocky outcrops, particularly after the autumn storms. Lichens populate tree bark, soil and rocks. Along the coastline that gets covered by water, lichens are responsible for the dark, almost black colour of the rocks. Higher above sea level, lichens adorn the rocks with green, yellow, orange and brownish colours.

State of the forests

Currently, woodlands and forests cover almost 7,500 km^2, or 36% of the surface of Euskal Herria. This gives an idea of the importance of the woodlands in the country's landscape, economy and culture. In the provinces of Bizkaia and Gipuzkoa, more than half of the terrain is woodland, although most of the coppices are planted with exotic, fast-growing species, such as insignis pines and eucalyptus trees. In Araba, Navarre and Ipar Euskal Herria, the area covered by woodlands is less extensive but the forests are natural, with beech being the most common species.

Euskal Herria also preserves a peculiar type of forest that once existed in other European regions as well. We are referring to the forests of beeches that have been pruned to make their trunks short and thick, with a large number of branches stemming from them, instead of allowing them to grow tall and thin (they can reach a height of 40 m).

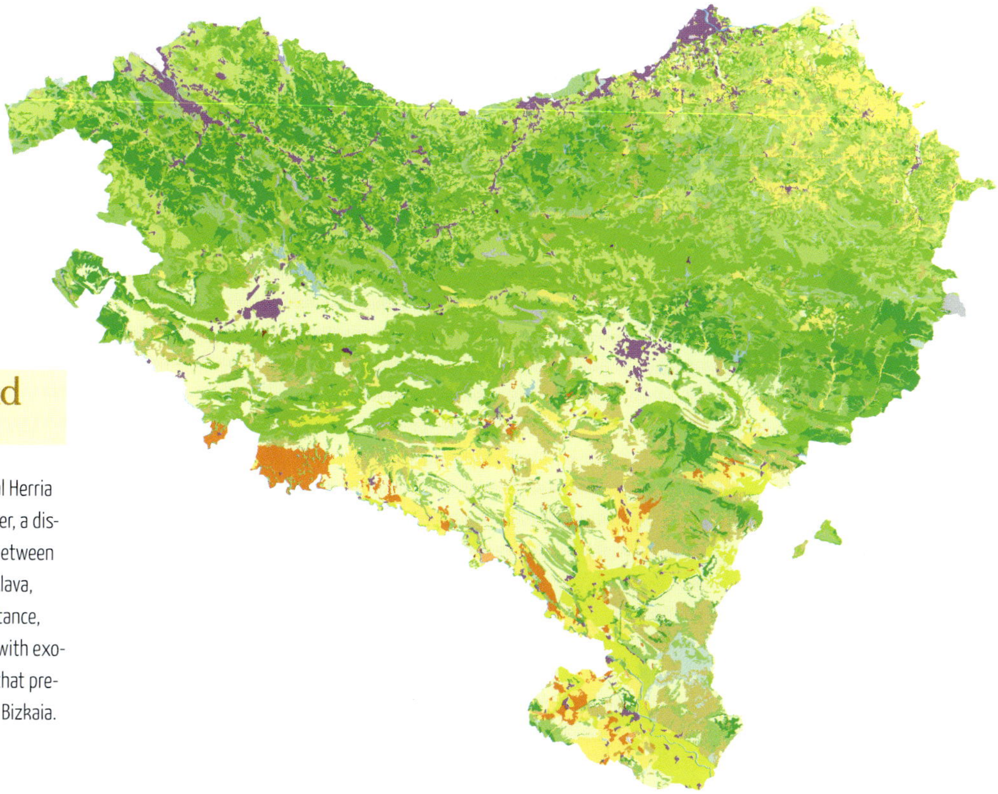

Forests and coppices

More than a third of Euskal Herria is covered in trees. However, a distinction should be made between the extensive forests of Alava, Navarre and Soule, for instance, and the coppices planted with exotic, fast-growing species that predominate in Gipuzkoa and Bizkaia.

ARTIFICIAL AREAS:
- Urban, industrial, commercial and transport areas

AGRICULTURAL AREAS:
- Farmlands
- Permanently irrigated land and rice fields
- Permanent crops (vineyards, fruit orchards and olive groves)
- Heterogeneous agricultural areas

FOREST AREAS OF NATURAL VEGETATION AND OPEN SPACES
- Coniferous forests
- Deciduous forests
- Areas of shrubs and/or herbaceous vegetation
- Open spaces with little or no vegetation

AREAS OF WETLANDS AND SURFACE WATER

Source: Gaindegia.

Forests of Euskal Herria

Oak | Insignis pine | Beech

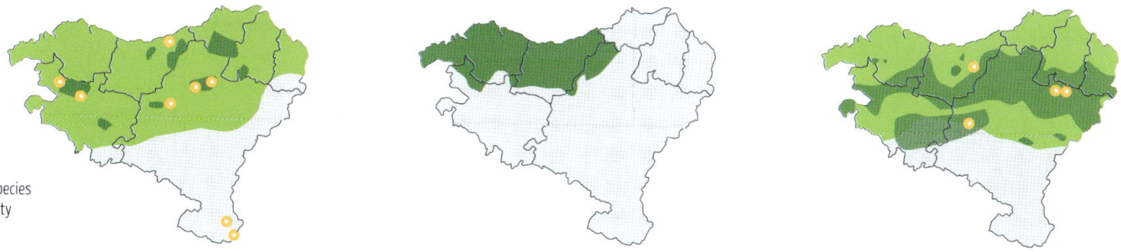

- Natural area of the species
- Areas of higher density
- Singular tree

Mushrooms

An excessively popular pastime

Mushrooms are very common in Euskal Herria, but unfortunately not so common as the habit of collecting them, a pastime that is linked to another highly popular pursuit: hiking. Mushrooms appear in spring and summer, but mostly in autumn, after a rainfall. They mostly grow in the shade of deciduous forests, like the charcoal burner mushroom (*urritxa*, one of the most common species); green brittlegills (the popular *gibelurdin*); chanterelles, penny buns, clouded agaric (*ilarraka* or *pago-ziza)*; Caesar's mushroom and the sweet tooth mushroom. Saffron milkcaps, bloody milkcaps (native to pinewoods), sticky buns, Boletus aereus, bay boletes, March mushrooms and wood blewits grow in the fir forests. Wild mushrooms, Scotch bonnets, king trumpet mushrooms, *galanperna* and St. George's mushrooms (the *perretxiko*) grow in the meadows and heathlands. So much exuberance has been diligently added to the outstanding Basque cuisine.

It is a well-known fact that hunting wild mushrooms can result in illness or even death. Some dangerous species that grow on Basque soil are imitators of harmless species, such as the highly poisonous livid pinkgill and the woolly milkcap, as well as the *Russula emética* and *Boletus satanas*. The danger increases with the *Amanita muscaria* or fly amanita, and the deadly amanitas: the death cap (*Amanita phalloides*), fool's mushroom (*Amanita verna*) and European destroying angel (*Amanita virosa*).

A land of BIRDS, WILD BOAR and CETACEANS

The wild animal life in the Basque Country is neither abundant nor diverse, perhaps because the country is small and has been inhabited since long ago. In general, the best preserved species are birds, small mammals, reptiles and insects. To the contrary, large mammals are scarce or nonexistent in most of the country, although a few endangered species are being reintroduced. The fact that the inhabitants of many towns are known by the name of an animal gives an idea of the importance that animal life has had in the Basque culture. The people of Bilbao are known as the *txinboak* (Eurasian blackcaps) and of Galdakao as *mozoloak* (little owls). The people of more than a dozen towns in Alava and Idiazabal, in Gipuzkoa, are known as *azeriak* (foxes). The townspeople of Amezketa are *euliak* (flies).

The return of wild boars

A few large animals still remain in the natural areas of the green, Atlantic Euskal Herria. Wild boar has prospered in recent decades, having benefited from diminished livestock grazing and a decline in the forest industry. Red deer have been reintroduced in the Gorbeia mountains and roe deer in the Urdaibai. Wolves, absent for decades, are reappearing sporadically in Karrantza and the Gorobel/Salvada mountain range, coming from the province of Burgos. Smaller animals include foxes, badgers, weasels, moles, dormice, squirrels and hedgehogs. Reptiles are represented by green lizards, common wall lizards and a variety of snakes, from the Aesculapian snake and grass snakes to the Baskian viper.

The wetlands in this part of the country are home to amphibians such as the common salamander, palmate newt and several species of frogs and toads.

Land birds have witnessed the return of birds of prey. Currently the most common ones are common buzzards, kestrels, little owls and common owls. Other birds worthy of note are swifts, wrynecks, Eurasian jays, sparrows, European goldfinches and song thrushes, as well as species that have become part of the local

Wild boar has returned to most of the country in recent years.

Greylag gooses.
A migrating flock.

folklore: callous cuckoos, robins (*txantxangorri*), (lovers of scrublands), common blackbirds (*zozos*, increasingly frequent in urban parks) and Eurasian wrens (the amusing *txepetx*).

Several species of seagulls, cormorants, northern gannets and terns fly in the skies of the coastal area, along with other less well-known species, such as the storm petrels that seek refuge on the islands of Biscay/Bizkaia. The coastal wetlands of Urdaibai, Txingudi and Urdazuri are where thousands of birds set off on their seasonal migrations, including many Anatidae, herons and egrets.

Survivors

Wild boar, a species whose only enemies are humans, have also increased their presence in the Mediterranean area. The most common carnivores are foxes, badgers and weasels, as well as European polecats, beech martens, genets and wild cats. The critically endangered European mink can still be found in a few spots in southern Araba and Navarre. There is an abundance of rodents, bats, moles and shrews, as well as populations of Pyrenean and Iberian rabbits and hares.

Reptiles proliferate, from common salamanders to western three-toed skinks and several types of ophidia, including ladder snakes, viperine (or water) snakes, Montpellier snakes and snub-nosed vipers. We also boast a small treasure in the form of the only two species of turtle found in the Basque country: European pond turtles and Spanish pond turtles. Mediterranean amphibians are represented by marbled newts and several types of toads.

A complete list of birds would be excessively long. However, we cite a few commonly found birds of prey: kites, kestrels, western marsh harriers, falcons and Bonelli's eagles. Storks, black crowned herons, mallards, partridge, quail, moorhens and many other species also abound. A few specimens of bustards, a bird that can be up to one metre in height, reside on the prairies of the Bárdenas Reales, in Navarre/Nafarroa. Thousands of birds congregate in the wetlands of Guardia and Uribarri-Ganboa, in Araba; and Las Cañas and Pitillas in Navarre/Nafarroa in certain seasons.

Where bears once roamed

The Pyrenees are the oldest area in the country and boasts the greatest biodiversity. In fact, some species are represented by only a few specimens restricted to very small areas. One of these is the karst area in Larra and environs in the northwestern tip of Navarre, at an altitude of 1800-2440 metres above sea level. A few species manage to survive in the harsh subalpine climate of that territory, including rock ptarmigans and wood grouse, although the latter are very scarce. The last native bears of the Pyrenees have been detected within the same area, as in the case of Camille. Other bears have been reintroduced, like Nere. They come from the Central Pyrenees and are only spotted occasionally, although no sightings have been documented in recent years.

As everyone knows, bears are symbolic and atavistic in the European culture. In the Basque context, they have been a carnival figure in parts of the Pyrenees, as in Arizkun, in the Baztan valley. Another typically Pyrenean bird of great symbolic importance is the golden eagle, the *arrano beltza* on the seals of the first monarchs of Navarre. A few pairs live within Navarre, Zuberoa and Lower Navarre and another small group away from the Pyrenees, in the Izki natural park, in Alava. The Pyrenean chamois, a nimble bovid who defies the law of gravity as it leaps from one outcrop to another has found its last stronghold in Larra.

Other large mammals in the Pyrenees are wild boar, roe deer and red deer. The calls of the red deer during the rutting season can be heard in the beautiful Irati forest and a few other places. The carnivores include foxes, badgers, weasels, European polecats, beech martens,

Two storks watch
over their nest.

A red deer and her fawn in the
Salburua wetlands (Araba)

A fisherman casting a line into the crystal-clear water of the river Leitzaran (Gipuzkoa)

genets and wild cats, as well as animals with delicate skins, such as stoats, otters and pine martens. The most frequent rodents are garden dormice, bank voles, Mediterranean pine voles and marmots. The latter was introduced in the mid-twentieth century. Hares are the most common of the lagomorpha. The insectivores include moles, common shrews and water shrews, and the Pyrenean desman. Reptiles such as the common lizard, green whip snake and the poisonous European asp; and

A pair of European bee-eaters

amphibians such as the salamander, common frog, Pyrenean brook salamander and European tree frog complete the list.

Finally, among the bids we can cite the golden eagles, rock ptarmigans and wood grouse, as well as many birds of prey and scavengers, including kites, kestrels, vultures, northern goshawks, booted eagles, short-toed snake eagles and Montagu's harriers. Egyptian vultures and, most of all, bearded vultures are among the endangered species that are on the increase. Other birds include partridges, quail, turtle doves, pigeons, little owls, eagle owls and green woodpeckers. The Passeriform clade of birds in the Pyrenean habitat is so plentiful that the list would be endless: crows, magpies, Eurasian jays, choughs, alpine sparrows, chaffinches, alpine goldfinches and so forth. The Pyrenean passes of Lindux and Organbidexka are the perfect vantage points for observing the passage of thousands of birds in spring and autumn. They are not for bird watching alone. Hunting blinds are distributed all along the Pyrenean ridges. Hunting with nets, a method used only in Euskal Herria, is still practised in Sara and Etxalar. The narrow passes of Arbaiun and Burgi boast the best positions for watching birds of prey.

Freshwater fish

The Basque Country's rivers are not the best examples of biodiversity but the situation has improved over the past few years. Pollution has decreased, especially in the rivers on the Atlantic watershed where trout, rainbow trout (an American species used in hatcheries), barbels, *Achondrostoma arcasii* (termed the *bermejuela*, in Spanish) and *Parachondrostoma arrigonis* (a type of carp).

The estuaries of the Atlantic rivers give life to species such as the righteye flounder, flathead mullet, three-spined stickleback and freshwater eels. Eel reproduction is an amazing adventure. At a certain stage, adult eels leave the rivers and cross the Atlantic ocean to the Sargasso Sea, where they spawn and die immediately after. The ocean currents drive the young eel larvae back to European coasts, where they enter the estuaries and travel upstream in freshwater rivers. That is how the expensive, sought-after eels arrive in our estuaries at the mercy of the tides and the moon.

Something similar, but in the opposite direction, is the habit among the salmon that live in the river Bidasoa, sea trouts and allis shad. In other words, are born in fresh water, migrate to the ocean and then return to fresh water to spawn.

Similar species inhabit the upper course of the rivers on the Atlantic watershed: trout, *Rutilus arcasi*, freshwater eel and *Phycis blennoides*. The species that live in the middle and lower courses include the gudgeon, carp, tench, barbel, Achondrostoma arcasii and goldfish.

The star among the river animals is the crayfish, a crustacean that lives in the rocky beds of crystal-

clear water. The crayfish are critically endangered due to pollution, intensive fishing and competition from the American red crayfish, introduced in the 1970s, which carried a disease against which the native species had no defences. Only a few crayfish survive in some of the headwaters that the invasive species cannot reach.

From anchovies to whales

Despite the intensive fishing that has driven many species to extinction and decimated many others, the Bay of Biscay still holds many life forms, from marine invertebrates such as polyps, jellyfish and annelids to the large cetaceans. Small molluscs live in the sand and rocks along the coastline, including horn shells, limpets, St Jame's shells, thick top shells, mussels, razor shells and clams. Cephalopod mollucs such as octopuses and squid share the same habitat. Diversity is the hallmark of the crustaceans as well. They range from Daphnia, goose neck barnacles and striped soldier shrimp to crabs, velvet crabs, spider crabs and other species that are highly esteemed as seafood. Starfish, sea urchins and sponges can be found in the shallower seabeds.

Fishing, the traditional occupation along the Basque coast, has caused some species to disappear, such as the *Balaena Biscayensis*, a whale native to the Golf of Biscay. The last large cetacean hunted by Basque fishermen was a whale spotted in front of the Orio sandbar in 1901. Fishing has also caused a drastic reduction in the numbers of many other species, although measures have recently been taken to preserve the threshold of survival. There is also a negative aspect to those measures, however: the fishing industry is declining in the Basque Country.

The most sought-after fish for commercial purposes are anchovies and sardines, which reproduce on the Cantabrian coast in spring and winter, respectively. Another popular fish is albacore tuna, a white tuna that spends the winter on the Azores and enters the Golf of Biscay in summer. It is a cousin of the Atlantic bluefin tuna, highly appreciated worldwide, which enters the Golf of Biscay in summer.

Several species of cetaceans, including rorquals (pictured), sperm whales and whales are frequent visitors to the Basque coasts.

Other abundant species are the Atlantic horse mackerel and other mackerel, whereas the populations of hake and sea bream have dwindled dramatically. Sea bass, which live rocky areas and the mouth of rivers, also swim in Basque waters, along with pouts, Mediterranean rainbow wrasse, red mullets, scorpion fish and anglerfish. The Basque inshore fishing fleet organises its sorties in accordance with the migratory habits of the main species. In March they wait for the mackerel; in June they fish albacore tuna and Atlantic bluefin tuna.

The cetaceans are the largest inhabitants of Basque waters. Some marine mammals, like dolphins and porpoises, live off the Basque coast permanently, whereas many others are seasonal, like whales, sperm whales, orcas and rorquals. Whale watching cruises are organised from the ports of Bermeo and Zumaia.

Domestic animals and native breeds

Humans have been accompanied by domestic animals that facilitate their existence since prehistoric times. Some domestic animals, such as dogs and sheep, even interacted then as they still do in the Basque mountains today. As in the rest of Europe, dogs appear to be the first domesticated animal. Some native canine breeds have been preserved, like the Basque working dog known as the *villano*, from the region of Las Encartaciones. Sheep have formed a substantial part of the landscape in the main mountain areas since the Neolithic Period. Many of

the mountain ridges were deforested to provide pastures for the flocks. A shepherd culture was developed that still survives today. In the humid Euskal Herria, the latxa or manex breed of sheep predominate. Their wool is rough but they produce a lot of milk. Churra sheep (also known as *rasa navarra*) are raised for their meat in the dry areas of the country, and so are some merino sheep. Goats and, above all, cattle were also domesticated. The traditional breed of cattle is the Pyrenean cow –*betizu*– (*Bos taurus*), with varieties such as the *terreña* and *monchina* cattle raised in the western part of the country. Accustomed to living in semi-freedom for centuries, the *betizu* cattle population has been drastically reduced to a few hundred heads of cattle distributed throughout the Basque mountains. Currently, the most widespread cattle are the Holstein and Swiss breeds, rather than the traditional Pyrenean breed. Pigs are mostly stabled on farms and industrial undertakings. Farmers often raise one or two pigs to feed their families, as well. Two of the native breeds have disappeared: the Baztan pig and the snub-nosed *chato* pig from Alava. In contrast, the Basque pig known as the *euskal txerria*, of which there were only 25 specimens in Lower Navarre in 1989, has proliferated and extended its range to other provinces. Nonetheless, most of the pigs currently on Basque farms are crossed with the York, landrace, large white and pietrain breeds. A few native species of poultry have also been preserved, such as the *euskal oiloa*, a critically endangered Basque hen.

The mountains in some regions of the country are home to a breed of native horses known as *pottoka*, a tough breed of ponies raised in semi-freedom.

On the preceding page, a Betizu cow, Basque hen chicks, a Carranzana Cara Negra sheep and a Basque sheepdog. Above, a Pottoka horse.

kostaldea, costa, côte

coast

Wild sea in Biarritz (LAPURDI).

Beach and flysch rocks in Zumaia (GIPUZKOA

kostaldea, costa, côte
coast

The beach in Deba (GIPUZKOA).

Jaizkibel (GIPUZKOA).

Steps leading up to San Juan de Gaztelugatxe (BIZKAIA).

A vintage piece of artillery from the cape of Billao (GORLIZ, BIZKAIA).

A sailing boat off the Basque coast.

Outcrops in the Duranguesado (BZKAIA).

Ascent to Hiru Erregeen Mahaia (NAFARROA).

mendiak, montes, montagnes mountains

Gorobel-Sálvada (AR

Boulders on the Behorlegi mountain (NAFARROA BEHEREA).

Natural window in the Leire mountains (NAFARROA).

mendiak, montes, montagnes

mountains

Mist and mountains rising above the Irati forest (NAFARROA BEHEREA).

Sharp rocks in the Kodes mountains (NAFARROA).

The port in Lekeitio (BIZKAIA).

Artaxoa with its walls (NAFARROA).

herriak, pueblos, communes

towns

The Alzola neighbourhood (AIA, GIPUZKOA).

Detail of a house in Ainhoa (LAPURDI).

herriak, pueblos, communes
towns

Zarautz in the mist (GIPUZKOA).

Portugalete and the transporter bridge (BIZKAIA).

Errezil (GIPUZKOA).

Euskal Herria in RESERVE

To preserve at least a part of the biodiversity we have mentioned in the preceding paragraphs — i.e. flora and fauna as well as landscapes, water and territories — some areas have been protected by legal mechanisms granted by governments and even international institutions. We begin with the biosphere reserves and then take a tour of the nature parks.

Urdaibai

The first Basque biosphere reserve was designated by a UNESCO committee in 1984. The Urdaibai Biosphere Reserve, located close to Gernika, boasts 220 km^2 of territory characterised by the extensive marshes of an estuary that has not been channelled. Thousands of birds flock to the reserve every year. It boasts a spectacular coast and dense forests of Cantabrian oaks cover around 1,350 hectares of its mountains. The island of Izaro, the only one on the Basque coast large enough to be a proper island, lies within the reserve. In addition to being a biosphere reserve, parts of Urdaibai are also protected as Special Areas of Conservation (SACs), Special Protection Areas for birds (SPAs) and Sites of Community Importance (SCI). One of the most protected areas is the islet of San Juan de Gaztelugatxe and the area surrounding it.

Mouth of the Gernika estuary with the island of Izaro in the background

Las Bardenas

The other biosphere reserve is in La Ribera, in Navarre. It is Las Bardenas Reales, 42,500 ha of semidesert landscape designated as a biosphere reserve by the UNESCO in 2000. It had been declared a natural park by the government of Navarre one year earlier. Las Bardenas boasts three clearly differentiated areas: El Plano, consisting of farmlands; Bardena Blanca, which is mostly desert with some prominent peaks such as Pisquerra, which have withstood the fierce erosion; and Bardena Negra, where Aleppo pines and scrub cover the parched soil. Deep ravines, isolated hillocks and green oases such as El Vedado de Eguaras dot the landscape. Thousands of sheep come down from the Pyrenean valleys to graze on the prairies in autumn. Surprisingly, a 2,222 ha shooting range

Sand, marshes and extensive oak forests covering the slopes are the main treasures in Urdaibai.

Naked slopes ravaged by erosion in Las Bárdenas

Nature reserves and Parks

Euskal Herria boasts two biosphere reserves recognised by the UNESCO (Urdaibai and Bárdenas), as well as a dozen nature parks declared as such by the autonomous governments.

for war planes, used by the Spanish army and occasionally by NATO since 1951, still survives in the heart of the reserve.

Natural Parks

The Basque government and the government of Navarre have designated several nature parks in recent years. Here you have a bird's eye view of them. We start with the Gorbeia Natural Park in Araba-Bizkaia, consisting of more than 260 km2 of protected land in the Gorbeia mountain area. It protects such unique spots as the Goiruri waterfall (height, 85m), the Altube beech woods (2,000 ha) and the stony heart of the Natural Park: the karst area in Itxina. The Urkiola Natural Park in Araba-Bizkaia safeguards such emblematic places in Basque mythology as the Anboto mountain, the Baltzola cave and the natural bridge of Jentilzubi; not to mention the sharp limestone ridges in the Duranguesado region. In the Encartaciones region of Bizkaia, Armañón Natural Park extends along a limestone massif dotted with caves — some as large as cathedrals — and covered by native forests.

In Gipuzkoa, the natural park of Pagoeta has turned its vantage point on the coast into a small universal botanical garden (Iturraran), while recovering its original forests at the same time. The Aralar natural park is much more ambitious. It includes a large area dedicated to herding on the mythic summits of Txindoki-Larrunarri, surrounded by the natural beech wood on the Lizarrusti pass, the most extensive forest in Gipuzkoa. Aizkorri-Aratz (Gipuzkoa-Araba) is a large park (194 km^2) where sweeping beech woods, rocky karst outcrops like Deguria, and the renowned Urbia meadows surround one of the country's

Wind and water have moulded the peak of Castildetierra

most important religious and cultural sites: the Arantzazu shrine. Last but not least, Aiako Harria is the only granite massif in a country saturated with limestone mounds.

The list continues with Valderejo (in Araba), an abandoned valley where a little stream has chiselled out a narrow pass to flow into the river Ebro. The Izki natural park in Araba stands out for its vast forest of Pyrenean oak and nearby rock caves in Markiz, which are part of an area known, rather pompously, as the Basque Cappadocia.

In Nafarroa, the Bertiz estate has been converted into a lovely botanical garden surrounded by a fully mature Atlantic forest. The Urbasa and Andia mountain ranges constitute another amazing natural park with large expanses of beech woods, meadows, underground caverns and such enchanting spots as the source of the river Urederra. Other areas under special protection in Nafarroa are the Ukderdi and Aztaparreta nature reserves, in the Larra-Belagua valley in the subalpine area of the country; and Lizardoia, a remnant of primary forest in the heart of the Irati forest.

In reference to the north Basque Country, the French government has included an extensive part of it in the Natura 2000 network. The protected area covers practically all of the northern slopes of the Pyrenees, from Larrun to the highest peaks of Zuberoa, as well as a large part of the Labourd coast between the bay of Txingudi and Biarritz, the estuary of the river Urdazuri and the beautiful Arbaila massif.

Beech woods in the Bertiz nature park (NAFARROA).

The natural eye of Aitzulo (Aizkorri-Aratz Nature Park in GIPUZKOA).

natural areas

Ballo mountain (ARABA).

The karstic massif of Itxina (Gorbeia Nature Park in BIZKAIA).

A path in San Kristobal (Izki Nature Park in ARABA).

Waterfall in the Valderejo nature park (ARABA).

natural areas

A POPULATED country

The roofs of the houses cluster around
the bell tower in the Fifth Parish (Bilbao)

At the turn of the twenty-first century, Euskal Herria's population reached the milestone of three million people. This is a modest figure compared to other European countries and states, even for those of a similar size. Even so, it is a milestone for a country that has not had a single city with more than 20,000 inhabitants for two hundred years.

If we divide the population uniformly between the country's 20,924 km^2, each square kilometre would have 150 people. This is an important population density that is exceeds that of neighbouring states (France, 117; Portugal 115 and Spain, 93). Logically, the population is not distributed uniformly. Bizkaia hosts 37% of the Basque population, followed by Gipuzkoa (23%) and Nafarroa (20%). Araba (10%) and Labourd/Lapurdi are one step behind, whereas Lower Navarre/Nafarroa Beherea (1%) and Soule/Zuberoa lag even further behind. There are two extremes: large conurbations and areas that are almost unpopulated. The main Basque cities are to be found close to the mouth of the river Ibaizabal, from Galdakao to Santurtzi, with Bilbao (population 351,000) being the largest city. The towns have grown until they have merged one into the other in continuous succession. One out of every three Basques lives in this area, where the population density is 3,700 inhabitants per km^2.

The other two large towns are Gasteiz (pop. 242,000, 75% of the population of Alava); Iruñea (197,000) and Donostia (186,000). In the French Basque Country/Ipar Euskal Herria, Bayonne/Baiona, Anglet/Angelu and Biarritz (BAB), population 120,000, constitute the main urban centre. Some areas are very densely populated and others are almost uninhabited. The harsh climate, isolation and the economic downturn in the primary sector in the foothills of the Pyrenees lowered the population to minimal levels in the mountain areas. Soule/Zuberoa has a population of just over 15,000 people (17 people per km^2), whereas the valley of Zaraitzu has barely 1,500 people in 310 km^2 (5 people per km^2). The least populated area is the eastern third of the country, where the tallest peaks in the Pyrenees and the Bardenas desert are located.

Elderly man sitting on a bench. Below, the city of Donostia stretches toward the sea.

Ancient and aged

The Basques like to believe that they are the most ancient people in Europe. As we will see, they have good reason to hold that belief. In any case, they are definitely among the oldest peoples. Or, at least, the most aged. In recent years, this small corner of Europe has experienced the same demographic phenomena that have characterised the rest of the developed world: a decline in mortality rates and a marked drop in the birth rate since the 1970s, outlining a scenario of little demographic growth and an ageing population (people over 65 represent 19% of the population).

Despite that, the capacity for generational renewal appears to be guaranteed. The main problem is observed in the small rural towns in the

less populated areas (such as the eastern valleys in the Pyrenees), where the percentage of ageing population is very high. There are few young people in those areas and they tend to migrate to the cities in search of a better life, making the future of the small rural towns uncertain.

Point of arrival and point of departure

In the nineteenth century, there was an explosion of capitalist development in Euskal Herria. After the Carlist wars, the mines on the left bank of the river Ibaizabal and later the steelworks and shipyards Bizkaia and Gipuzkoa attracted thousands of workers, mostly from other regions of Spain. The migrations started in the last quarter of the nineteenth century and continued into the twentieth century until the oil crisis in the 1970s. The population of Euskal Herria tripled in just under 100 years. The population explosion affected the four peninsular provinces at a different pace: first in Bizkaia and Gipuzkoa and later, in the 1950s and 60s, it reached Araba and Nafarroa. The population in Gasteiz, for instance, increased from 52,000 people in 1950 to 192,000 in 1981. It is estimated that more than half of the Basque population today descend from the people who came to the country during that period.

In the meanwhile, the three continental territories remained untouched by the industrial boom. The only alternative to farming, apart from the commercial area of Bayonne/Baiona, was tourism, which was made fashionable by Eugenia de Montijo, the wife of Napoleon III, emperor of France. The limitations of Basque agriculture forced part of the population to migrate on a regular basis. Interestingly enough,

Pedestrian avenue in Gasteiz. People of all ages strolling under the trees

Population density

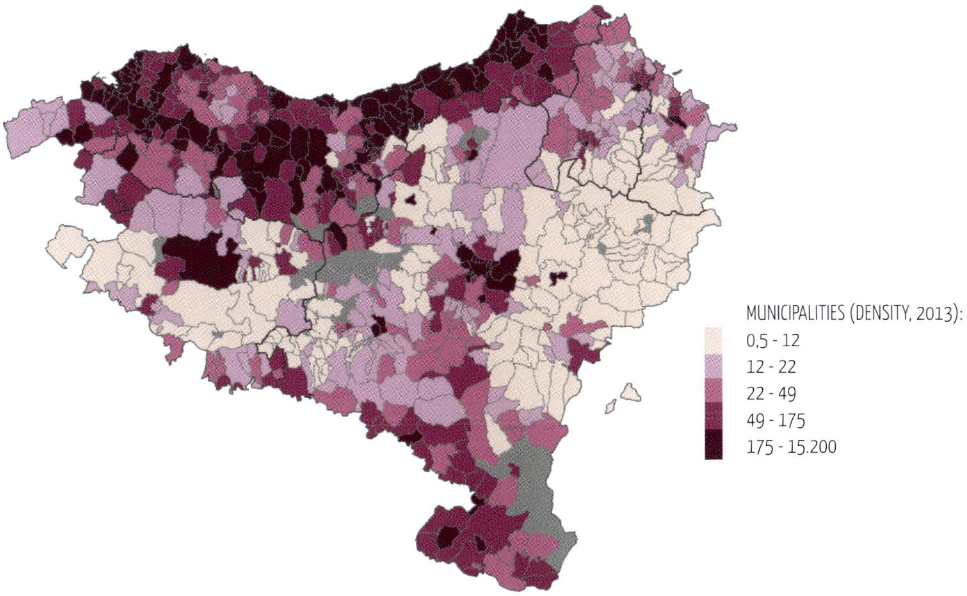

A map of the population of Euskal Herria shows the density by municipalities. The most populated cities and towns are on the coast, a few inland valleys in Bizkaia and Gipuzkoa and close to Gasteiz and Iruñea.

Source: Gaindegia.

Population growth

Euskal Herria, 1877-2013 (%)

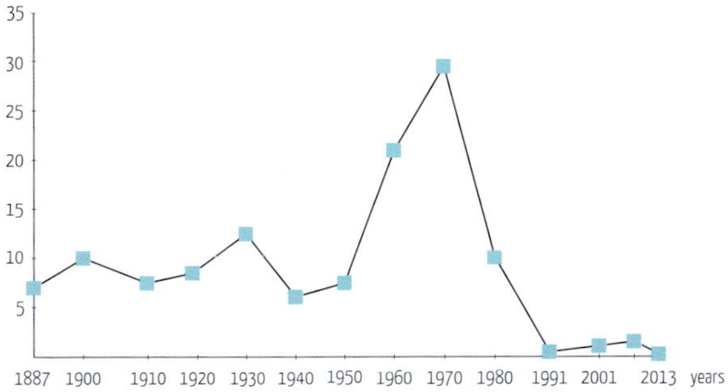

Source: Gaindegia.

Births, deaths and natural increase.
Euskal Herria, 1962-2004.

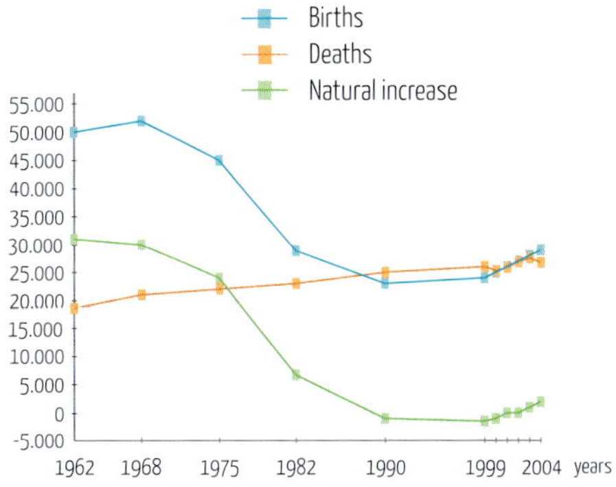

Source: Gaindegia.

By place of birth

Distribution of the population over the age of 15 by origin and parents' origin, by historical territories.
Euskal Herria, 2001 (%).

Source: Gaindegia.

ÁREA	Born in EH	Inmigrants	Inmigrants parents
Euskal Herria	50	25	25
Araba	40	29	31
Bizkaia	42	26	32
Gipuzkoa	54	22	24
Lapurdi	31	52	17
N. Beherea	54	32	14
Nafarroa	69	18	13
Zuberoa	72	20	8

in data

DISTRIBUTION OF THE POPULATION IN %

Bizkaia	37%
Gipuzkoa	23%
Nafarroa	20%
Araba	10%
Lapurdi	7,5%
N. Beherea	1%
Zuberoa	0,5%

the peninsular Basque territories were rarely the destination of the young people from the French Basque Country/Ipar Euskal Herria who were forced to leave their country. Most of them were drawn to America and later to Bordeaux and Paris. In the meanwhile, tourism brought thousands of people to the Labourd coast. Some of them stayed, generally on a seasonal basis; that is, they had a holiday home there. They still do.

At the end of the twentieth century, migration experienced a global surge that only the economic downturn in 2008 was able to slow down. The new Basques come from faraway countries now, and often from other continents. Many different susceptibilities, cultures, colours and languages have settled in this area of the Bay of Biscay.

Tribute to Basque immigrants on Ellis Island (New York, United States). Below, stamp and postal envelope of the Saint Pierre et Miquelon archipelago, which defends its Basque legacy

The eighth province

Ever since the early modern period, the Basque people have been departing from their country to earn their living or seek a better future. During the period of the *Fueros*, a Spanish word meaning "charter of rights, practices and customs", the land that had given birth to the Basques and their social organisation could only permit a limited population, so many men and women had to venture into the world with their few possessions. After the Spanish conquest, America became the destination of Basque emigration. Curiously, migration was reinforced after the Spanish American wars of independence in the nineteenth century. Fleeing from the Carlist wars, military service and poverty, many peninsular and continental Basques headed for Argentina, Uruguay and Mexico. Later they migrated to the United States, where they worked as shepherds in the twentieth century. The Spanish civil war (1936-39) brought about another massive diaspora, with America as the preferred destination.

Most Basques settled in their new countries permanently, leaving a trail of Basque surnames around the globe. Their descendants are counted by the millions worldwide, with varying degrees of awareness of their Basque past and identity. They are the diaspora, or the eighth province, grouped around *euskal etxeak* (Basque centres).

Others returned. Of those who did, one social group stands out: the *indianos*, or those who made their fortune in America and returned to end their days in their homeland. They were in the habit of building sumptuous mansions to show off their wealth.

Farms, hamlets and large towns

Traditionally, the distribution of Basques in the country has followed a few clear criteria. The population in the Atlantic area has always been dispersed. Basque farms and farmhouses are scattered over most of the land, except on the tallest mountains and thickest forests. Sometimes they are grouped into neighbourhoods, but always with some distance between them. Some of the farms have huts on the tallest mountains, where the shepherds spend part of the year with their livestock. Interestingly enough, the largest Basque conurbations have developed precisely in the areas of dispersed population.

In the middle section of the country that runs through Araba, Nafarroa and both sides

The hamlet of Torralbal del Río (Navarre) surrounded by cereal crops, in the shadow of the Kodes mountains. Below, the new buildings are taller than the churches in the small towns that surrounded Gasteiz.

of the eastern Pyrenees, the settlements began to merge, although they are still very dispersed. The farms in the valleys are grouped together, forming hamlets at short distances from each other, instead of being scattered on the slopes and along the river banks. The capitals of the two provinces, Gasteiz in Araba and Iruñea in Nafarroa, are located in this transition area.

The population becomes denser further south. The farms and hamlets gradually disappear, giving way to larger towns separated by kilometres of croplands. The Ribera region in Nafarroa is a good example of this.

INDUSTRIAL territory

An ancient legend ascribes the merit of acquainting the Basque people with the secrets of metallurgy to a hero named Sanmartintxiki — Saint Martin, according to Christian doctrine —, after using his ingenuity to steal the knowledge from pagan giants. What is certain is that metal has formed a part of Basque life since olden times, producing the steel to make the famous Toledo swords, setting up foundries in the early modern period, and blast furnaces in the nineteenth and twentieth centuries. Currently, at the start of the third millennium, the country has adapted to new times while retaining, against all odds, an industrial framework that employs almost 34% of the work force. That is the highest employment rate in Europe. In many valleys on the Atlantic slopes, farms, factories, roads and cities follow one another incongruously, making up an anarchic landscape that is sometimes grotesque and other times simply incredible.

The iron and steel industry was one of the pillars of the country.

The perennial crisis in the primary sector, more critical than ever

In the early twenty-first century, agriculture, livestock-raising and fisheries are looking for their survival as productive sectors in Euskal Herria. It is becoming increasingly difficult to live off the fields, animals and the sea. While technical advances make certain tasks easier, their profitability is uncertain, at best. In addition, rural land has been affected by the spiral of speculation that the boom of the brick caused up until the housing bubble burst in 2008. In the northern half of the country, livestock holdings are still important in Nafarroa Beherea, Zuberoa and the Atlantic part of Navarre, while they have lost much of their weight, although they have not wholly disappeared, in Bizkaia, Gipuzkoa and Aiara region of Alava. Most of the production is milk and meat, of both sheep and cows. On the contrary, the vegetable gardens serve a local market share that is increasingly difficult to maintain. Small scale producers (almost all the industry in this part of the country) react to the downturn by betting on quality. This has led to the consolidation of *txakolin* wine, beef, beans,

and the cheese from Idiazabal, Irati-Ossau and Roncal. In the southern half, the holdings are larger and farming carries more weight, thanks to the good name of their wines (Rioja Alavesa and Navarre), potatoes (Araba), cereals (Araba and Navarre) and garden produce like asparagus, peppers and other vegetables (the Ribera region in Navarre). The most productive branches are pig farms (Navarre) and poultry (Araba).

In reference to another sector, the Cantabrian ports have undergone major changes in the last 30 years, to the point of becoming unrecognisable. The wharfs that literally had no more room for the inshore fishing fleet in the late 1970s are seeing the fishing activity disappear from the docks, which are now occupied by pleasure boats. Ondarroa (Bizkaia) and Pasaia (Gipuzkoa) still maintain their deep-sea fishing activity, while inshore fishing barely survives in a few ports like Bermeo and Ondarroa (Bizkaia), Getaria and Hondarribia (Gipuzkoa) and Ziburu/Ciboure-Donibane Lohizune/Saint-Jean-de-Luz (Labourd). The hardness of the work and obvious decline in catches due to overfishing have driven the industry to a critical point. However, key species such as the anchovy have begun to show signs of recovery.

From large factories to small workshops

A striking feature of the Euskal Herria of the early twenty-first century is the significant persistence of an outstanding industrial fabric that is both flexible and dynamic. This is still a country of factories. Industry is concentrated in the metropolitan area of Bilbao and the basins of the rivers Ibaizabal and Nervión, in the valleys of Gipuzkoa and the industrial belts of Gasteiz and Iruñea. In the French Basque Country/Ipar Euskal Herria, the main cities and towns are in the Baiona area and on the coast, although there are far fewer than in the rest of the country.

Above, an oil company terminal in the Abra (Zierbena, Bizkaia). Below, farming in the valley of Olatz (Gipuzkoa)

The economic downturn in the 1970s and 80s led to the dismantling of most of the steel factories in the country, including the blast furnaces, as well as a large part of the shipyards. Both sectors had been the base of industrial development in Bizkaia

Industrial activity

The adjacent map shows the country's main industrial regions and type of activity. The valleys of the Nervión-Ibaizabal rivers stand out in Bizkaia, and the valleys of the Deba, Urola and Oria in Gipuzkoa. Iruñea, Sakana, Gasteiz, Tutera and Bayonne complete the picture. The main activities are related to automobile parts, machine tools and metal. The canning industry in La Ribera, in Navarre, is also important. The fishing ports are also shown.

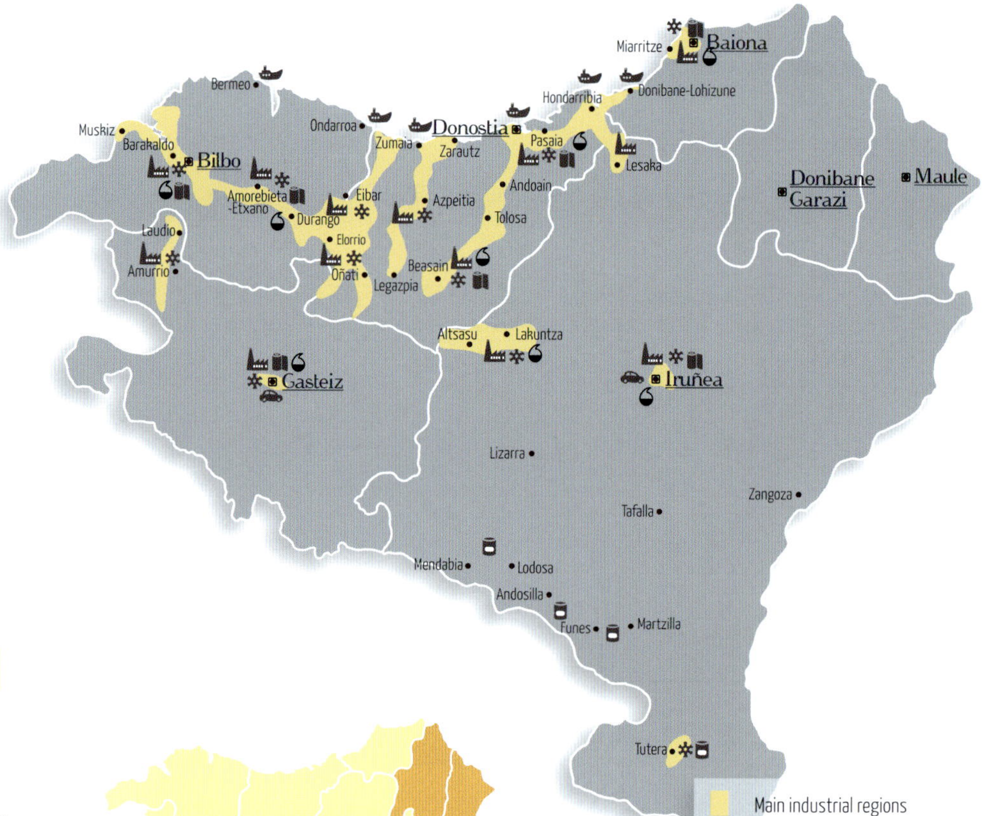

Primary sector

Currently there are two provinces in which the primary sector still employs more than 10% of the population. These are Lower Navarre/Nafarroa Beherea and Soule/Zuberoa, although they are the less populated provinces. Agriculture and livestock raising are still important in large areas of the country, but normally they are combined with other activities in the industrial or services sectors.

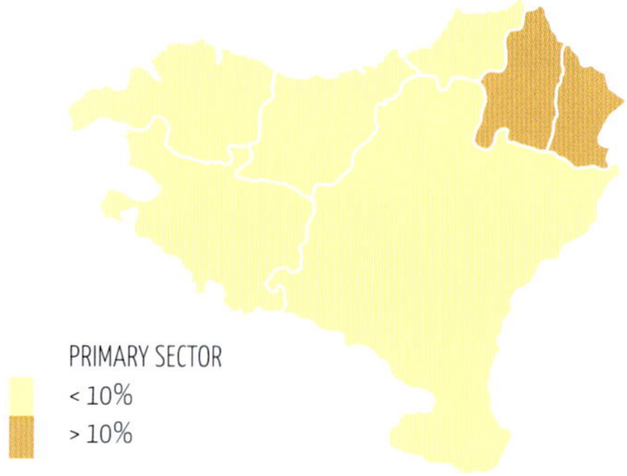

Balance of trade

BALANCE OF TRADE	2000	2002	2004	2006	2008	2010	2012
Euskal Herria	4,32	2,7	1,76	-0,59	1,87	6,05	8,33
Finland	9,1	9,2	6,5	4,7	3,8	1,3	-0,6
EU-27	0,2	1,5	1,2	0,5	0,3	1,0	2,0
USA	-3,8	-4,0	-5,2	-5,8	-5,0	-3,5	-3,6
Japan	1,4	1,3	2,0	1,3	0,2	1,2	-2,0

Source: Gaindegia.

Unemployment rate

UNEMPLOYMENT RATE	2000	2002	2004	2006	2008	2010	2012
Euskal Herria	12,08	7,75	7,30	4,86	4,92	9,81	12,85
Finland	9,80	9,10	8,80	7,70	6,40	8,40	7,70
EU-27	8,80	8,90	9,30	8,30	7,10	9,70	-
USA	4,00	5,80	5,50	4,60	5,80	9,60	-
Japan	4,70	5,40	4,70	4,10	4,00	5,10	-

Source: Gaindegia

Note: The unemployment rate in Euskal Herria was 16.7% in July 2014.

Above, technology park facilities in Zamudio. Below, a sidewalk café full of customers. Tourism is an industry with a future.

and Gipuzkoa, along with the now defunct iron mining. Today only a few large companies with more than one thousand workers remain, whereas in the past they were common. The Volkswagen factories in Landaben, in Iruñea (6,000 workers) and Mercedes Benz in Gasteiz (3,000 workers) are the last survivors of that type of production. In their place, countless workshops and small and medium-sized enterprises constitute the bulk of the country's industrial fabric, especially in Gipuzkoa. Many of the companies are set in the cooperative sector, the world's most powerful sector in its genre, although the crisis that started in 2008 has also made a dent there. The commitment to technological research and R&D was one of the reactions to the crisis of the 1980s and can be seen in technology parks like those in Zamudio (Bizkaia) and Miñao (Araba). The development of branches such as heavy machinery, machine tools, capital goods, automobile parts, aeronautics and steel is particularly significant. The global crisis opened in 2008 has increased existing phenomena such as relocation, compounded by a fall in demand.

Services, the new rulers

The oil crisis and conversions of the 1980s drastically reduced industrial employment. The adverse situation reinforced the service sector, which had been less relevant before then. In 1975, 53% of the population worked in industry, whereas services gave employment to 38%. As in much of the western world, Euskal Herria was also driven towards the tertiary sector. Commerce, finance, transport, telephony, culture, tourism, education and health, together with the public administrations, formed a heterogeneous amalgamation that was employing three out of every five Basques in 2001.

Thus, the loss of momentum in the fishing ports contrasts with the consolidation of three large commercial harbours, Bayonne/Baiona, Pasaia and Bilbao, authentic references in Atlantic Europe's maritime traffic. Trade in the capitals (including cities like Biarritz) represent a significant economic sector in

which small traders have lost their prominence to the big brands and chain stores.

Tourism is a typical example of the growth of the tertiary sector. If the infrastructure of services was minimal in the 1980s and was concentrated in the traditional summer resorts of Donostia and the Labourd coast, 30 years later practically every town has rural accommodation, hotels, apartments and camping grounds, not to mention tourist offices, tourist consortiums and tourist packages for leisure and holidays. Services are a global phenomenon from which Euskal Herria has not retreated.

capitales, hiriburuak, capitales

capitals

Euskalduna Conference Centre, on the banks of the river Ibaizabal, in BILBAO.

DONIBANE GARAZI street.

The castle in MAULE.

The walls of the citadel guard the best park in IRUÑEA.

capitals

Monument to the battle of 1813, in the centre of GASTEIZ.

Colourful shutters on the windows in BAIONA.

Bay and promenade of La Concha (DONOSTIA).

Numerous horses decorate the walls of the Ekain cave (Zestoa, Gipuzkoa)

An OLD European people

In terms of their origin, the Basque people are unique, since they have no known relatives and their origin is still a matter of debate. That is why Prehistory is one of the areas where scholars look with the hope of clarifying mysteries. No definitive answers have emerged to date, but while we persevere in our search, we are surprised to find some treasures and quite a few enigmas.

A series of stalactites in Izturitze (Nafarroa Beherea)

Human beings appear

The dawn of humanity in present day Euskal Herria goes back at least 200,000 years. That is the age calculated for the oldest findings made so far on Basque soil: a string of utensils carved from stone with the shape of the Acheulian culture that appeared in the alluvial plains near Iruñea (Navarre/Nafarroa) and Bidaxune (Lower Navarre/Nafarroa Beherea); in caves (the Lezetxiki cave in Mondragón/Arrasate) and the open air settlements (in Sopela, Bizkaia). However, scholars believe that the human presence may have been earlier and more extensive because the only human remains found in the Basque area that could have belonged to that period is the Lezetxiki humerus. It appears to belong to *Homo heidelbergensis*, the predecessor of the Neanderthals, who existed relatively nearby, in Atapuerca, in the province of Burgos.

The Middle Palaeolithic Period was more generous, leaving a heritage of many archaeological sites; some human remains, like teeth belonging to the Neanderthals (*Homo neanderthalensis*) in Lezetxiki, Axlor and Arrillor; and tangible culture. The population of Euskal Herria during that period (100,000--40,000 BC) formed small communities of hunters-gatherers whose technological development was far superior to that of their predecessors, to judge from their tools. They knew how to make fire and used certain rituals to bury their dead. Most of their remains have been found in the Atlantic Euskal Herria.

Grandiose first art

The Stone Age reached its peak with the Upper Palaeolithic Period (40,000-10,500 BC). It was a predominantly cold period that, therefore, has left its traces in the more temperate zones on the

coastal and less elevated areas of the country. More than one hundred archaeological sites have been found within the current boundaries of the Basque Country, all of them ascribed to the new species of human being, *homo sapiens sapiens* or Cro-Magnon, which then spread worldwide. A series of caves from Karrantza (Bizkaia) to Zuberoa have preserved the earliest, most extraordinary examples of rock art, which the experts have classified as Franco-Cantabrian art. The bison of Santiamamiñe (Bizkaia) and Altxerri (Gipuzkoa); the horses of Ekain (Gipuzkoa) and the engravings and hundreds of pieces of portable art in Izturitze (Lower Navarre/Nafarroa Beherea) are the crown jewels of the large legacy to posterity left by the primitive communities.

Metals and megaliths

The warm climate during the Mesolithic Period (10,500-5,000 BC) allowed humans to expand across the rest of the country, which until then had been at the mercy of perpetual snow that in some periods started at altitudes

Dolmen in La Chabola de la Hechicera, including its gallery, in Elvillar (Araba)

Neolithic dolmen cromlech ancient castles Ilarrita

of only one thousand metres. The sea, to the contrary, advanced several kilometres inland. The Neolithic Period followed, somewhat later (5,000--2,500 BC) in the current Basque territories than in other parts of Europe. Agriculture emerged, as well as grazing. These activities became more widespread in the era of metals. In the Chalcolitic Period (Copper Age), humans stopped living off nature alone, hunting, fishing and gathering. The population growth forced them to sow and breed whatever they wanted to eat. That led to the animal husbandry, linked to the country's mountains, that has endured, with logical updates, until the present. During the Bronze Age (2,000 BC), the communities became more complex as the megalithic culture spread, especially among the stock breeders who took over the hill ranges. There are more than 800 dolmens scattered through the seven territories, from Guardia (Rioja Alavesa) and Artaxoa (Navarre) to Karrantza (Bizkaia) and Soule/Zuberoa. The first open air settlements had sprung up, while new populations arrived at this end of the Pyrenees, leaving their Indo-European influence. The phenomenon increased in the Iron Age (1,000 BC), when walled forts were built at low altitude in the southern part of the country, and at the top of cliffs and hills in the central strip and northern half. In the French Basque Country/Ipar Euskal Herria they are known as *gazteluzahar*, ancient castles. The Indo-European presence became more entrenched, while cromlechs (a circle of stones, at a low height in the Basque case) replaced the dolmens as the preferred burial rite in the Pyrenean area. Today we can enjoy such magical spots as Ilarrita, one of the great necropolises in the Pyrenees, formed by twenty-six cromlechs scattered over a grassy slope of Mount Okabe, in Lower Navarre/ Nafarroa Beherea.

The cromlechs extend all along the Pyrenees mountain range. Surprisingly, at the Basque end, the western boundary is currently marked by the right bank of the river Leitzaran, in Gipuzkoa. That is to say, in all the territory west of the Leitzaran, cromlechs do not exist or are virtually non-existent. This has led some researchers to hypothesize that the territory of the cromlechs corresponds to a particular people which the Latin sources identified as a Vascones.

Dolmen of Jentillarri (ATAUN)

Dolmen of Mairietxe (MENDIBE)

Menhir on the Adarra mountain (ANDOAIN)

megaliths

Crómlech of Oianleku (OIARTZUN)

Dolmen of Sorginetxe (AGURAIN)

Dolmen of Farangortea (ARTAXOA)

Menhir of Soalar (BAZTAN)

megaliths

Ruins of the Roman city of Andelos (Mendigorria, Navarre). Below, earthenware jugs in the Roman museum of Oiasso (Irún, Gipuzkoa)

When the Romans arrived

This is the situation that the Romans found. It is one of the many mysteries that Basque history has left us. Leaving assumptions aside, we have yet to establish a reason for the abrupt end to the cromlechs, which seems to point to a profound cultural rift in the land that is now Euskal Herria. Furthermore, the tribes that inhabited the peninsular part of the country when the Romans arrived have not been clearly identified. Some researchers defend the pre-Indo-European nature — and, more specifically, the Basque nature — of all or a part of the tribes indicated by the Latin authors of that period: the Vascones, Vardulii and Caristii. The other two, Autrigones and Berones, are questionable, particularly the latter, who are usually labelled as Celt. Authors of prestige, like José Miguel Barandiaran, have endorsed the continuity of the population within the current Basque borders since the Neolithic Period.

Another current sustains the hypothesis of a late Vasconization, according to which a part (mainly, Bizkaia, Gipuzkoa and Araba) or all of the peninsular Basque territory was inhabited by Indo-Europeans until the Vascones from the northern foothills of the Pyrenees took it over in the sixth century, after the fall of the Roman empire. Curiously enough, French academics have defended the opposite hypothesis for a long time, namely that the abundant Basque imprint in Aquitaine was caused by invasions or movements of people from the southern slopes.

In any event, recent research on the Roman period has revealed a very different picture from

what was perceived thirty years ago. On the one hand, the Romanization of the *ager vasonum* (the flat farmlands on the Mediterranean side of the country) and the *saltum vasconum* (mountainous regions) was more intensive than previously thought. There were settlements, factories, cities and small towns in a large part of the country. On the other hand, the Basque people entered into the history written by the Romans and, surprisingly, in an area not currently Basque: Aquitaine, in the broad area between the river Garonne and the Pyrenees. Numerous graffiti found there abound in Basque-like words. On the contrary, fewer written testimonies of a Basque nature exist south of the Pyrenees, although they do exist outside of the present-day Basque territory, as shown by the ones found in La Rioja.

A substantial change

The Roman period substantially transformed the face of present-day Euskal Herria, especially owning to the technological advances in agriculture, urban planning, mining, navigation, art, communication channels and so forth. All this also meant an expansion of an economic model based on large estates

Installations in the Roman villa of Las Musas (Arellano, Nafarroa)

Roman mosaic in Arellano (Navarre) and sculpture found in the ruins of Veleia (Iruña de Oka, Araba)

and slave labour. In any case, during the more than five centuries of domination (1 BC to 5 AD), the Romans erected the first cities, including Veleia, in Iruña-Oka; Pompaelo, in Iruñea; Foru, in Bizkaia; and Andelos, in Mendigorria; as well as garrisons like Lapurdum, in Bayonne; ports like Oiasso, in Irun; and saltworks in Getaria, both in Gipuzkoa and Lapurdi. They settled in large estates (latifundia) such as the ones in Ledea/Liedena and Ramalete in Tudela; mines like the Arditurri mines in Oiartzun; and mapped out roads that crossed the country, such as the Asturica-Burdigala road from Astorga to Bordeaux.

Today we can enjoy a part of that legacy. You can stroll through the streets of Veleia or by the hot springs of Andelos; do down the Arditurri mines or ascend to the round tower of Urkulu, which looks out over the Pyrenees from an elevation of 1,400 meters. The Roman museum of Irun, the mosaics of Liedena, the goddess found in Foru and the newly discovered Iturissa, near Auritz-Burguete are part of a modest but interesting list. The Roman period has left an extraordinary treasure, with a convenient touch of mystery: the surprising persistence of the Basque language, one of the few native languages that survived the Roman Empire, and the only pre-Indo-European language.

The first Basque political structure

During the twilight of the Empire, while urban life was declining and the Roman world became more rural, successive waves of Germanic peoples crossed the Pyrenees. Most of them were violent. Towards the end of the Roman Empire, the Basques, too, were raiding neighbouring territories. At first they were gangs of fugitive peasant brigands identified as Bagaudae, although apparently not specifically Basque. Later, assault detachments that the chronicles identified as Vasones led the attacks. In those turbulent years, the few historical references to Vasconia imply that its population sought to remain on the sidelines of the two great powers that had been organised around them: the Visigoths of Toledo and Narbonne, and the Merovingians who had settled in Paris. Both powers sought to bring the Vascones under their control. In this context, the Basques of present-day Euskal Herria and those of Aquitaine — who had left so many pseudo-Basque epigraphs five centuries earlier — were merged by the Merovingian monarchy into an incipient political structure known as the Duchy of Gascony (also Vasconia) (602-768), which stretched from the banks of the river Garonne to Bizkaia and Araba. The Aquitanian Vasonia, intensively Romanised, ultimately led to Gascony. It should come as no surprise that the burials of this period found in Araba (in Aldaieta) exhibit a great relationship with the Frankish culture and none with the Visigoth. During this period there were constant clashes with both cultures, inside and outside of the Basque territory. Visigoth and Frankish chronicles refer to a barbarian, untamed people. The Muslim chronicles mention that the last Visigoth king, Rodrigo, was fighting the Vascones in Iruñea when he heard of the Mohammedan invasion of the Iberian Peninsula (711).

The Kingdom of Navarre, from Orreaga to Sancho the Great

The onslaught of the troops of the Caliphate to Damascus occupied most of the Iberian Peninsula and the county of Narbonne in a few years, until they were detained in the battle of Poitiers (732), on the banks of the Loire. Since then, the current Basque territory was confined between the Muslims, who replaced the Visigoths as powerful neighbours to the south, and the Franks. The heirs of Charles Martel, the victor in the battle of Poitiers, organized a new empire in Western Europe, under the aegis of Pepin and, with the title of Emperor, under aegis of Charlemagne. The Basque tribes, characterized globally in the chronicles as Vascones, soon had to cope with the pressures of both colossi, the Carolingians Franks and the Emirate of Cordoba. Over time, several strategies were devised, from collaboration and even marriage, to direct confrontation. The confrontation went down in history as the famous battle of Orreaga or Roncesvalles, one of the first historical examples of propaganda that turned the defeated into heroes and wiped out the victors. The *Chanson de Roland* immortalised Charlemagne's nephew and eliminated the Vascones, who were replaced by some dangerous Saracens, who the authors of the song undoubtedly considered to be a more important enemy. However, what is certain is that the attackers were Basques, that there was a second battle of Orreaga in 824 against another Frankish army with the same outcome, and, above all, that both battles had a significant impact. Shortly after, in the early ninth century, a small political framework, created under the command of Enneco Arista (Eneko Aritza, in Basque), became the Kingdom of Pamplona and later, the Kingdom of Navarre. The monarchs with authentic Basque names (Eneko, known as Artiza, the oak) attempted to group the Vascone populations under their rule, an ambition that faced competition from the Frankish power in the north and the incipient Christian kingdom of Asturias in the west.

In the midst of weddings, alliances, raids, fully fledged attacks and obscure events, the new kingdom managed to free itself of Carolingian tutorship and collaborated or confronted the adjacent kingdoms, whether they were Christian and Muslim. Maximum splendour was attained under the rule of Sancho III the Great (1004-1035), when the monarch expanded the traditional Basque territories — with the exception of the Ribera of Tudela, the agricultural region of southern Navarre, still under Islamic rule — to include the counties of Aragon,

Late 15th century tapestry depicting the battle of Orreaga (Roncesvalles) as a confrontation between Moors and Christians.

Sobrarbe and Ribagorza, in the Pyrenees; parts of Castille; and La Rioja, where Basque was still spoken in those days. Upon his death, Sancho III left a kingdom for each of his sons: Navarre, Castille and Aragon. In a few years, his legacy

was divested, the victim of internal strife and skirmishes with the neighbours.

In the meantime, two far-reaching events were taking place. One was the arrival of the Vikings, whose settlement in Bayonne/Baiona in the ninth century has been confirmed. They may also have landed at other points along the coast of Bizkaia. They even kidnapped García Iñiguez, the king of Iruñea, who was only released after payment of a sizeable ransom. The Vikings did not leave the coast of Aquitaine until they were forcibly evicted at the end of the tenth century. Some scholars are of the opinion that the Basques' nautical skills in subsequent centuries was caused by their contact with the invading Normans. Whatever the reason, the truth is that the coastline of Euskal Herria began to have more importance that it ever had before.

The other far-reaching event of that period was the feudalization of the country. Both the Visigoths and the Franks had evolved into societies based on serfdom, fiefdoms and vassals. The Basque population arrived at the same type of social organisation, although with important nuances, depending on the region.

Wars of clans

In 1076, while Castile occupied one part of Navarre, the rest was under the rule of Sancho I of Aragón, who was also the king of Navarre under the name of Sancho V. His son and successor, Alfonso I the Battler took Tudela and its Ribera from the Muslims (1119). Alfonso I died without offspring, which paved the way for Pamplona to regain its own monarch instead of sharing one with Aragon. The monarch was García Ramírez, who went down in history with the nickname of the Restorer. Navarre flourished anew under Sancho VI the Wise (1150-1194) but with no possibility of expanding southwards at the expense of the Muslims. It was sandwiched between its two powerful neighbours, Castile and Aragón, which at the end of that same twelfth century agreed to apportion the former Vascone kingdom. The monarchs of Navarre founded the cities of Vitoria-Gasteiz (1181) and Donostia-San Sebastian (1180) to build up the kingdom's defences. It was not enough. In 1200, a Castilian attack Navarre lost Araba, Gipuzkoa and the Duranguesado. The rest of Bizkaia was already within the Castilian orbit, although without being part of the kingdom.

Leonor of Aquitaine and her son John Lackland in a mural in the church of Sainte Radegonde in Chinon (France)

Maps of that period show Navarre as a small kingdom constrained among others that aspired to become giants. The Vascone settlement had been reduced to present-day Navarre, the Rioja Alavesa and, on the other side of the Pyrenees, Lower Navarre/Nafarroa Beherea. To the east lay Aragón; to the west, Castile; to the north, the English domains of Aquitaine (including the Basque territories of Labourd/Lapurdi and Soule/Zuberoa), Aquitaine being the result of the marriage between Leonor of Aquitaine and

Engraving depicting the capture of a whale

basque nobility
sabelgorriak
Sancho
Middle Ages
Aquitania

Henry Plantagenet in 1054. Bizkaia, converted into a feudal estate, was allocated to the heir of the crown of Castile in 1371, as the result of another marriage. Although the kingdom of Navarre and the feudal estate of Bizkaia retained their separate political structures, the country was already completely divided between the powerful medieval monarchies of Castile and England.

In the twelfth century, the Basque coast began to show signs of vitality. New activities emerged, such as whale hunting, and the inlets and estuaries were fitted out for anchorage. Aside from the fishing activity, the Cantabrian ports were included in the trade route that linked Castile to England and the Netherlands. The bays of Biscay and Gipuzkoa were ideally suited to become active agents in that trade. Half fishing ports and half merchant towns, in the following years Bilbao, Bermeo, Getaria and Donostia grew to a prominence that before would have unimaginable. The coast of Labourd, under the sovereignty of the English monarch, retained its importance, with Bayonne, the only Basque port that remained active throughout the Middle Ages, being the main point of reference.

However, the late medieval crisis that hit Europe with its trail of pandemics also reached Euskal Herria, causing a similar response: the violence of the lords. The country experienced a period of civil strife in which the noble lineages confronted their troops, which had formed large *bandos*, or clans: the Oñaz and Ganboa clans in Bizkaia, Gipuzkoa and part of Araba; the Agramonte and Beamonte clans in Nafarroa; the Marroquines and Salazares in Las Encartaciones; and, in the seventeenth century, the *sabelgorriak* and *sabelzuriak*, in Labourd/Lapurdi. The clans formed coalitions: the Oñaz with the Beamonte clans and the Agramonte with the Ganboa clans. They laid waste to the country in an attempt to demonstrate who was more important and to increase their income, which the global crisis had seriously diminished. Although the end of the clan wars is generally presented as a defeat of the bellicose Basque nobility, they actually maintained their power and control over the population until the eighteenth century, making it not so clear that they were the losers. The impression may be due to the fact that the Castilian monarchs, allied with the towns, forced the Oñaz and Ganboin clans to dismantle the top parts of their defensive towers, and outlawed the clans in a process which obviously led to the strengthening of the real power. It also heralded a new but successful legal status: universal lesser nobility, by which all the inhabitants of a region were considered nobles by birth and equal before the law, at least in theory. The system was established for Bizkaia, Gipuzkoa and several of the valleys in Navarre, such as Baztan, Zaraitzu and Erronkaribar. At first glance, it seemed to be a victory of the bourgeoisie and the popular classes against the hegemony of the clans. To some extent, it was. However, it may also have been an adaptation of the feudal nobility to the new conditions, because universal gentry laid the foundations for their new ideology in the early modern period: the ideology of the Fueros.

Jauregizarrea, tower of Arraiotz (BAZTAN)

San Salbador church, in Getaria (GIPUZKOA)

Muñatones tower. Muskiz (BIZKAIA)

Cave dwelling in Gaubea (ARABA)

Necropolis of Argiñeta. Elorrio (BIZKAIA)

Witnesses of the Middle Ages

Paintings in Alaitza (ARABA)

Gares bridge (NAFARROA)

oad of San Adrian (GIPUZKOA)

The conquest of Navarre

During the Late Middle Ages, the old Vascone kingdom turned to France, which gradually grew closer to the Basque territory. In 1449, the French monarchy conquered Soule/Zuberoa in the context of the Hundred Years' War. One year later Labourd/Lapurdi was captured, although Bayonne/Baiona resisted until 1451. It was the last town in Aquitaine to fall into French hands. Thus English domination came to an end, having begun 300 years earlier, in the times of Richard the Lionhearted. Shortly after, Navarre was

Engraving of the taking of Iruñea during the conquest of Navarre

trapped between France, which as booming after the Hundred Years' War, and the new Spanish monarchy that had joined the crowns of Castile and Aragón, conquered Granada and landed in America. At the dawn of the early modern period, France and Spain were disputing hegemony in Europe. In 1512, Ferdinand of Aragón, the widower of Isabella of Castile, invaded Navarre. The king, leading the powerful army of the Duke of Alba, counted on the invaluable collaboration of the Beamonte clan, and used a crude ploy to justify the invasion in the form of a papal bull to excommunicate the monarchs of Navarre for being schismatic. The small kingdom fell fast, between July and September, although the fall was soon succeeded by three attempts to restore the independence (1512, 1516 and 1521). The most important attempt was the last one, because it succeeded in pushing the Castilians out of most of Navarre, including the capital, in only two weeks. The counter-offensive culminated in the battle of Noain, where the Navarre cause was lost. Other places also resisted, but the troops of the Emperor Charles V reconquered the entire region. The castle of Amaiur (in Baztan) and the fortress of Hondarribia (in present-day Gipuzkoa) were the last bastions to fly the flag of the Kingdom of Navarre. The monarchs withdrew to their properties in Gascony, where they recovered the Navarre on the north side of the Pyrenees (Lower Navarre/Nafarroa Beherea), abandoned by the Spanish monarchs. One of their descendants, Henry IV of France, became the first Bourbon to unite the crowns of Navarre and France (1594), after he declared, "Paris is well worth a mass", although there is some doubt whether he said this.

Painting by Alava-born Fernando Mendieta, depicting the Ferdinand V, king of Castile, vowing the rights of Bizkaia The text is written in Basque.

Two monarchies, seven Fueros

In the early modern period, therefore, the Basque territories were framed in two monarchies: the Spanish monarchy (Bizkaia, Gipuzkoa, Araba and what was known as Upper Navarre, or simply Navarre), and the French monarchy (Labourd, Soule and Lower Navarre or Nafarroa Beherea). Although most of the territories had been conquered, they arrived at agreements by which their ancient laws, or Fueros, were to be respected. The two Navarres, the Upper and the Lower, remained kingdoms, with their own courts and laws. The rest of the territories, each with its peculiarities, reformulated their status to bring it into line with the new situation

As the early modern period progressed, the two monarchies initiated centralising policies by which the laws of some of the countries they governed were abolished, as in Catalonia and Aragón. Thus, on the eve of the French Revolution, the Basque Fueros were the only laws that remained in force. In the case of the Fueros of Navarre and Bizkaia, the only connection with the monarchy was that they shared the same lord or monarch. Therefore, in the opinion of some scholars, the two communities maintained their sovereignty, at least in theory. Others, however, sustain that they the Fueros were remnants of feudalism and lacking in content.

In any case, the Fueros were not a trivial matter. Throughout the early modern period they governed the relationship of the Basque communities with the monarchies and constituted a framework of coexistence and conflict within those same communities. Most of the Basques who left their country could argue that they were of the lesser nobility, which implied access to important privileges in a class-based society.

A country that leans toward the coast

The sixteenth century marked a definitive shift of the country toward the coast. At the service of the imperial power of Castile, Bizkaia and Gipuzkoa supplied ships and sailors to the fleets that communicated the Indies with Flanders. The first galleons were built in their shipyards and equipped with the most advanced technology of the time. They have even been compared to twenty-first century spacecraft, relatively speaking. The first European whalers to fish in Newfoundland in the early modern period sailed from the ports of Biscay, Gipuzkoa and Labourd/Lapurdi. They set up factories and contacted with the natives on the Canadian island. Over time, the Basque sailors turned to fishing cod and plundering enemy ships. The territories governed by Fueros made sure that, in the event of war between their sovereigns (a situation that was all too common), the conflict would not ruin their relations. Bizkaia, Gipuzkoa and Labourd signed many conventions in the sixteenth and seventeenth centuries to secure their mutual neutrality in such battles. Some conventions were more effective than others, it is only fair to say. In addition to Bayonne, Donostia and Bilbao also became major cities within the country, although they did not exceed the size and population of the two inland capitals, Gasteiz and Iruñea.

In this period, some produce that arrived from America revolutionised the country's agriculture, customs and cuisine. Corn was well suited to the humid Atlantic climate, as were potatoes, although the latter could be grown on higher ground. Chocolate was introduced in France via Bayonne and tobacco provided sizeable profits to those who were engaged in the noble art of smuggling. Other local products attained fame and economic importance, especially the iron manufactured in hundreds of ironworks (artisanal workshops) along the riverbanks in the Atlantic valleys.

Despite universal nobility and the relatively democratic nature of some of the Foral institutions, society was still one of conflict in which the descendants of the noble clans, conveniently connected with the thriving merchant bourgeoisie, still laid hands on the peasants' surplus produce as they had been doing for three hundred years. Clashes occurred, as some British historians pointed out for their country, when the subordinate classes were wronged in their status as consumers. The Basque revolts during the Foral period, generally known by the name of *matxinada*, were often for that reason. The clashes included the Salt Tax mutiny in Bizkaia (1631-1634); the revolts in Baiona (1641) and Soule (1661) against unfair taxes; the customs revolt in Bizkaia and Gipuzkoa (1718); the *matxinada* of 1766 against the decree of the freedom to set prices, in Bizkaia and Gipuzkoa, and so forth. To these we should add the Zamakolada in Bizkaia (1804), against the military service. In all these cases the clashes were caused by laws that went against the letter and the spirit of the Fueros. In every case there were also other interests at stake.

The bay of Pasaia in a 19th century illustration

Garat
carlists
fueros
nationalism

Battle of Irún (Carlist war) in 1837

The stormy transition to capitalism (1789-1876)

The transition to capitalism was not easy anywhere in the world, but it was especially traumatic in Euskal Herria. In less than a hundred years the country experienced five wars, three of which were devastating, as well as many revolutions. In 1789, the French Revolution led to a Jacobean centralist state that, in the name of freedom, equality and fraternity, abolished the laws of every country under their domination and imposed the French language. It has been estimated that almost half of French citizens did not know the newly proclaimed, mandatory language, including most of the Basques in Labourd, Lower Navarre and Soule. The Fueros were repealed and the three territories became part of a newly created département, close to the province of Bearn. Shortly after, Basques on both sides of the border fought among themselves in the Convention War (1794-1795), either in the armies of Spain's Catholic monarch (the Spanish *Tercio* from the four peninsular provinces) or in the new national French army, which included the units known as the *Chasseur Basques.*

Attack against the Carlists by the French Legion.

Defences of the bay of Pasaia during the Carlist wars.

Siege and bombardment of Donostia in 1813

A Carlist ambush, with a priest leading the watch

The Convention War was a prelude to the Napoleonic invasion, which resulted in another war (1808-1814). Despite the fact that the two conflicts fuelled French and Spanish nationalism, they also led to the pro-independence movements, the first since the conquest of the Kingdom of Navarre three hundred years before. In 1794, a Basque assembly, the Juntas Generales of Gipuzkoa, called for the province to be constituted as an associated state of the French Republic. In 1803-1811, Dominique Joseph Garat, a politician from Labourd, promoted the creation of a Basque state that included seven provinces within Napoleon's empire. Both attempts came to nothing, but in 1810 the four peninsular provinces were split off from the Spanish monarchy unlawfully held by Joseph Bonaparte, Napoleon's brother, and integrated into the French empire.

The ensuing Spanish War of Independence ended with Napoleon's defeat, after some dramatic episodes, such as the Battle of Vitoria, to which Beethoven dedicated a symphony, and the attack on Donostia, when the Anglo-Portuguese troops set fire to the city in 1813. The Bourbons were reinstated on the French throne — although this time without the title of Kings of Navarre — and in 1812 a liberal constitution was drawn up for the Spanish monarchy in Cadiz, calling for the suppression of the Basque Fueros. The new constitution barely had time to be enacted before a coup d'état put an end to it and absolutism was restored. In 1820-1823, the years of the Liberal Triennium, another military coup reinstated the constitution and the Fueros were abolished again. Guerrillas rose up in defence of the absolute monarchy, religion and the Fueros, a trilogy that predated the foundations of Carlist ideology.

The final incorporation of the Basque territories peninsular to the new Spanish national state, with its unity of the market, army, parliament, judicial system and provincial constituencies required two more conflicts: the Carlist Wars (1833-1839 and 1872-1876), in which, under a dynastic issue in appearance - who would succeed Fernando VII- the transition to capitalism was decided. The main theatre of war was in the four provinces, for the most part dominated by the Carlist troops that the Spanish army was hardly able to defeat, even with the collaboration of France and England. In the two wars, the Carlists organised their own administrations (justice, police, postal service and so forth) on Basque soil, giving rise to a small state.

Workers and owners of the factory in Etxebarria (Bilbao) in 1896

Nationalism and socialism

The defeat of the Carlists meant the installation of the customs on the shoreline and the Pyrenees (until then they were on the river Ebro), the introduction of compulsory military service, the arrival of the judges of first instance, the abolition of the main Foral powers (like general meetings and legislation) and the liberation of productive sectors of great interest to capitalist development, which was taken over by a small oligarchy. Only the Basque Economic Agreement was saved, a new system by which the provincial councils collected taxes and then paid the State a negotiated amount called a quota. The method is currently still in place.

In the years immediately following, a part of the country changed completely. Thousands of people arrived in Bizkaia to work in the mines and the emerging steel industry. The first Bizkaian blast furnaces (1848) spelled the end of the old steelworks, which had become unprofitable. Mining and metallurgy expanded in Bizkaia and Gipuzkoa, given a fresh impulse to other industries, such as the shipyards. The workers' movement (1870) and Basque nationalism (1895) emerged as two separate spheres and the State responded with prison and repression. Sabino Arana, who founded Basque Nationalist Party and designed the *ikurriña* as the flag of Euskadi, experienced both. He was imprisoned for the first time in 1895, shortly after his revolutionary proclamation that the homeland of the Basques was Euzkadi.

lehendakari
Labour movement
Gernika
kastolak
ndependence

In the economic domain, other parts of the country followed different paths. Biarritz, like Donostia, became a summer residence for the aristocratic elite. Araba, Nafarroa and inland French Basque Country/Ipar Euskal Herria maintained their traditional agrarian structure, although not without conflict.

After the long parenthesis opened in 1876, the country knew no further episodes of war until World War I, when many young Basques from the French Basque Country/Ipar Euskal Herria had to fight with the French army. It is estimated that six or seven thousand of them perished. World War I and World War II (1939-1945) had a catalytic effect on the French attitude toward French Basque population, until then little identified with the State.

World War II was preceded by a dramatic event for Euskal Herria. On 18 July 1936, the greater part of the Spanish army revolted against the government of the Second Republic to impose a fascist regime. The uprising was a failure and led to a war. It took the same turn on Basque soil. The rebels counted on the support of the Carlists, who still ruled in most of the country, and the oligarchy. They took control of Navarre and much of Araba from the start. All the leftist forces and the Basque Nationalist Party opposed them, making the coup d'état fail in Bizkaia and Gipuzkoa. In October, the Parliament of the Spanish Republic adopted the Statute of Autonomy and constituted the Basque government, presided over by the *lehendakari* José Antonio Aguirre. The latter, in command of 45,000 men, resisted the attack of a far stronger enemy for eleven months. Among the bloodiest episodes of the war were the fascists' brutal repression in Navarre, (more than 3,000 civilians were shot, in a province where there was no war front); and the first bombings on civilian population in the history of Europe, with Gernika as the ultimate symbol, at the hands of the Luftwaffe of Nazi Germany, allied with Franco's forces. Three years later, in 1940, the Luftwaffe provided cover for the Wermacht to occupy France. Then they arrived in Hendaia. The French Basque Country/Ipar Euskal Herria was under Nazi rule until it was freed in 1944.

While the end of the Second World War resulted in the restoration of a democratic system in France, Spain continued under military rule for forty years. The dictatorship that emerged from the right-wing victory in the civil war, led by General Franco, ruthlessly purged all signs of Basque identity. Nationalist and leftist parties and demands were banned, and any expression of Basque culture that was not approved by Franco's regime was ruthlessly persecuted. Euskera was banned from the administration and schools, and the persecution even included churches and cemeteries. Strict measures were taken to ensure that the Basque language was restricted to the domestic sphere in the best of cases, i.e. between speakers who knew no other language, and never used in public or private institutions.

However, despite the frenetic repression, the regime could not erase the Basque identity. It was left in critical condition, of course, but the repression prompted a defensive movement that started with modest clandestine schools (*ikastolak*) that taught in the Basque language. Popular private schools were set up where adults could learn the language and illiterate speakers could learn to read and write it. Every field of Basque culture — dance, theatre and music — received an injection of vitality that prevented the language from disappearing and put it on the path to standardisation. This was a popular initiative that found no support from the official channels; only impediments and persecution, with few exceptions.

The momentum for renewal took root in the late 1950s. At the time, Bizkaia and Gipuzkoa

Euskal Herria
shaken

The aeroplane that carried the Nazi León Degrelle landing in La Concha (1945).

Basque women voting for the first time (Eibar, 1933).

Heinrich Himmler, commander of the SS, in a visit to Donostia (1940)

Refugee family on the beach in Hendaia (1936)

Company of Basque soldiers (1937)

Communist rally in Donostia (1935)

Jose Antonio Agirre on the Day of the Basque Homeland. 1933

were recovering the pulse of economic development. With metallurgy as their banner, the two provinces were still heading the country's industrial development, at a very high ecological cost. The first factory sites soon followed, springing up around Iruñea and the valley of Sakana (Navarre), the Gasteiz belt and the region of Aiara (Alava). Then came new clandestine organisations that would change the signs of the times. The first workers' committees were organised in the factories, on the fringes of the only legal trade union organisation in Francoist Spain. In Bilbao, a group of students founded ETA (the acronym for Euskadi ta Askatasuna, Euskadi and Liberty), a pro-independence organisation to the left of the PNV (Basque Nationalist Party) that adopted to crucial resolutions: to link the national struggle to the social struggle and to oppose the Franco regime in every way, including armed struggle.

The dictatorship's response was again brutal. The repression culminated in 1970 with the Burgos trials, in which several ETA militants were sentenced to death, and the shooting of Jon Paredes Manot, alias Txiki, and Angel Otaegi in 1975, a few days before Franco's death, along with José Luis Sánchez Bravo, Ramón García Sanz and Humberto Baena, who were militants in the Spanish communist organisation FRAP. ETA, for its part, was prepared to act ever more forcefully, as it showed in December 1973. Franco's right-hand man, Prime Minister Admiral Carrero Blanco was returning from daily mass when his car was sent flying into the air by some explosives detonated under the street. The prime minister died as a result of the explosion.

When Franco died, Spain faced a choice between reform and disruption. The first option won. It was called the "transition", that is, a step from the military dictatorship to a parliamentary system in a process safeguarded by the powers that be and without reviewing the past. The majority of Basque political forces advocated the right to self-determination, but the Constitution of 1978 established the unity of "the Spanish nation, the common and indivisible homeland of all Spaniards". The State also established the division of the four Basque provinces south of the Pyrenees into two different entities. In 1979 Bizkaia, Gipuzkoa and Araba became the Autonomous Region of Euskadi and in 1982 Navarre became the Comunidad Foral de Navarra (the Autonomous Region of Navarre). The two regions, as well as the provincial councils, enjoy broad powers in areas such as education, finance (the above-mentioned Economic Agreement), law enforcement (their own police forces, the Ertzaintza and the Navarre Regional Police), health and so forth.

Two pictures of Gernika after the bombings of 26 April 1937. The town that symbolises Basque freedoms was completely destroyed by the Condor Legion. For 40 years, the official version was that the "reds" set the town on fire before abandoning it.

From suffering to hope

In the following years, the State was able to group the majority of Basque political forces under its flag. The idea of a break with the Franco heritage remained in the hands of the *abertzale* (a separatist left or pro-independence group), which in turn included two political groups: the Herri Batasuna coalition and ETA, which maintained its commitment to the armed struggle approach in the new context. ETA carried out thousands of attacks, most of which were against the police and the military, but also against civilians or in which civilians were affected, both in Hego Euskal Herria (the southern, or peninsular Basque Country) and in the rest of the Spain. It is estimated that ETA caused more than 800 deaths in 1968-2009. Some of the attacks were directed against the civilian population, such as the explosion of a bomb in the Hipercor supermarket in Barcelona that killed 21 people. In the mid-1990s, ETA directed its armed activity against the elected members of some political parties, especially the PP (Spain's right-wing Popular Party) and PSOE (the Socialist Workers' Party). For more than a decade, thousands of politicians were protected by bodyguards.

The State never ceased to act forcefully. According to a report by the Basque government, 40,000 people (1.3% of the population) were arrested for political reasons in 1960-2012. At least 5,000 of these denounced that they had been tortured. Police forces and death squads, like the BVE (Basque Spanish Battalion) and Triple A units, which were active in the 1970s, and the GAL (Antiterrorist Liberation Groups), in the 1980s, killed around 200 people. The State changed its strategy in the mid-90s. It left the dirty war tactics in the background and opted for a loose interpretation of the laws under the axiom that "everything is ETA", in the sense that any person or organisation identified with the separatist left was liable to being accused of collaborating with ETA or being a member of the group. Thus, the State closed newspapers and a radio, prevented the presence of electoral candidates and outlawed political parties (including Herri Batasuna), as well as youth and social organisations.

Members of ETA condemned in a court-martial in Burgos (1970)

In the last few decades, there has been no shortage of attempts to achieve a negotiated peace, as the one brokered between ETA and the Spanish government in Algeria in 1989. In 1998, the Lizarra pact paved the way for another process that brought many moderate Basque nationalists and the *abertzale* left together for the first meeting in decades, but the pact floundered a year later. Lastly, in 2004-2007, ETA and the Spain, on the one part, and the PNV, PSOE and Batasuna, on the other, negotiated for months. The progress made in the negotiations gave rise to an internal reflection in the *abertzale* left that led to the Altsasu declaration in 2009, according to which the process would be exclusively peaceful and democratic. ETA endorsed the statement shortly after, in 2010, and in line with that decision took steps toward easing the hostility, such as the historical public announcement of a definitive cease to the armed struggle in October 2011.

The consequences of the armed conflict are far from being resolved and a democratic solution to the Basque question, or the political conflict, so to speak, is still pending. However, it is hoped that it will be resolved within the next few years, along different lines than those that have prevailed in the last few decades.

In this regard, it is fair to say that after the first elections were held after the death of Franco, the country's political blocks have remained consistent, with a few logical ups and downs. The moderately nationalist Christian democrat PNV and the separatist left (now grouped with other political actors into EH Bildu) are currently the majority parties, although closely followed by the Spanish right (PP and the UPN, a Navarre nationalist party that is contrary to any project in common with the rest of the country) and PSOE (the socialist party). In the French Basque Country/Ipar Euskal Herria, the right has always led the polls, followed by the Socialist Party. The *abertzales*, grouped into EH Bai, have managed to gain third place and around 15% of the votes.

Human chain for the right to self-determination that joined Durango to Iruñea (123 km), called by Gure Esku Dago in June 2014.

EUSKERA,
the lenguage of the Basques

In their own language, the Basques call themselves the *euskaldunak*, or "those who speak Euskera (Basque)". Therefore, anyone can become an *euskaldun* (a Basque); it is enough to learn the language. Apart from reflecting the open concept of belonging held by the Basque people throughout their history, the way of identifying themselves reveals the importance that this ancient people have attached to their language. We say "have attached" because, unfortunately, the majority of Basques no longer know their language. This may change soon, however.

A past for the Basque language

As occurred with many other languages, the Basque language was not spoken in the government institutions and the apparatus of power until the twentieth century. First came Latin, then the Occitan and Navarre Romance languages, then Castilian Spanish, and lastly, French. All those languages have served as the vehicle for government decisions, justice, education, property registries and even the last will and testament of those who knew no other language than Basque.

This was due, in large measure, to the inclusion of Basque territories in foreign monarchies. Yet it was not the only reason. The Kingdom of Navarre could have chosen Basque in the Late Middle Ages, but instead the Romance languages were used for official documents (Occitan, Navarro-Aragonese, Gascon and so forth). In the early modern period and the nineteenth century, the foral institutions could also have used Basque in their written communications. Instead, the ruling classes, the same who boasted of the antiquity of the language because it established the purity of their ancestry and lineages, imposed a knowledge of Spanish to participate in the General Meetings (territorial parliament) in Bizkaia (1630) and Araba (1682), despite, or perhaps because, most of the people did not speak it. Language was an instrument of power and Basque had the enemy at home.

The marginalization of the language in the administration and the prohibitions seem to have prevented the emergence of a social class that ordinarily wrote in Basque. Therefore, although written literature appeared in the sixteenth century, just like most European languages, it was not developed until well into the twentieth century

Absent from files and documentation, and lacking in a substantial volume of written literature, it could be said that the Basque language left hardly any traces of its past. The fact that Basque is not related to any other known language strengthens that impression. Basque survived the Indo-European invasions of the era of metals, Latinization of the Roman Empire, centuries of prohibitions, and even decades of persecution. If it had not been handed down to the present day, it might be thought that had not existed.

In the manuscripts in the monastery of San Millán de la Cogolla (Rioja) there are two annotations or comments in the margin, written in Basque in the 10th century. One reads "izioqui dugu" and the other (pictured) "guec ajutu ez dugu".

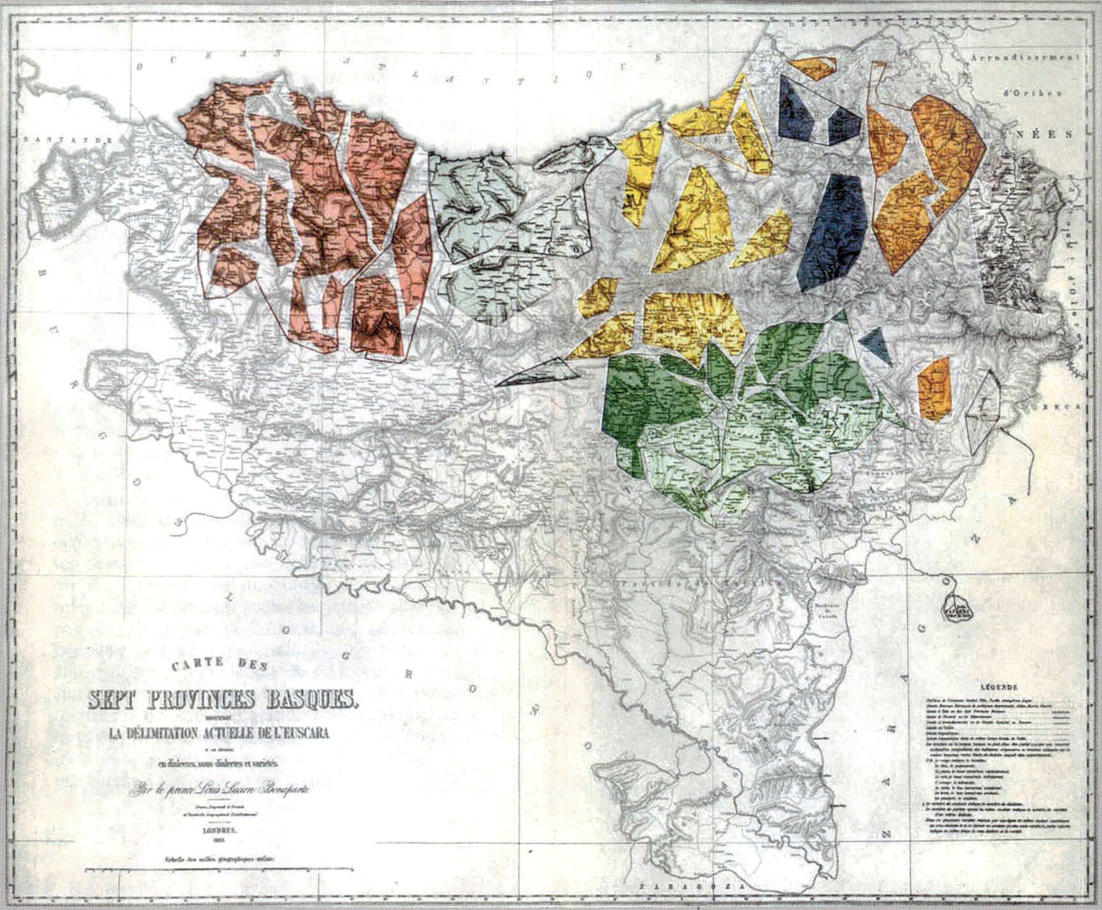

Map of the seven Basque provinces with the current delimitation of the Basque language. The year 1863. Made by Louis Lucien Bonaparte. Includes the limits of the dialects of Biscay, Gipuzkoa, two from the Upper Navarre and two from the Lower Navarre, Labourd and Soule .

But it has survived, in an extraordinary manner. Because it is one of the last remaining pre-Indo European languages, there are those who argue that it could come from the European neolithic language. In any case, there is no doubt of its remote past. Up to the eve of the twentieth century, most of the Basque people have lived in their language. They have used the Basque language to govern, sail across the seas, be identified in the new world, speak in the local assemblies, at parties, major events, in the streets of Bilbao and Iruñea, in their weddings and their funerals. The extraordinarily rich oral tradition has perpetuated a culture that can be traced back thousands of years. The Basque people have handed down the echoes of their ancient religion, their goddess Mari, a wide range of mythological characters and the clan wars of the Middle Ages via the Basque language. It is worth bearing in mind that the documents that populate Basque files are merely translations of real life into other languages. As Navarre-born historian José María Lacarra pointed out, "When writing the history of the Basque Country in the Middle Ages, we are constantly assailed with the worry that we are reconstructing the past of a people who write in a language that is not the language they speak, and that their language is escaping from them through the pages of the documents".

From yesterday to tomorrow

Today it is difficult to establish a map of the historical development of the Basque language with certainty. We know that until the Roman Empire it was spoke in a large part of Aquitaine, to the point that some researchers call the Basque language of that time the Aquitainian language. Linguists with the prestige of Joan Coromines have argued that Basque was spoken at that time and well into the Middle Ages throughout the western and central Pyrenees, as well as in the valley of Aran and Andorra. In the thirteenth century it was the everyday language in the Ojacastro valley, in La Rioja. However, at the dawn of the early modern period, Basque appears limited to the current territory of Euskal Herria, with two

exceptions. On the one hand, there were areas where the majority of people spoke the Romance languages, in some cases since the old days, as in the west Encartaciones in Bizkaia; the valleys of Alava around the river Omecillo; El Romanzado and La Ribera in Navarra; and Bastida in Lower Navarre). On the other hand, the Basque language crossed the border and penetrated Béarn and, perhaps, the Ansó valley, in Huesca.

The experts say that the dialects of Basque (*euskalkiak*) emerged in the Middle Ages, mostly as the result of the political collapse of the country. By the end of the twentieth century the dialects had reached a point where they made communication between Basques difficult, a fact that has weighed heavily on the country. The younger generations of Basques till today have never been literate in their language. The exclusion of the Basque language from the administration, education and spheres of power created the perfect conditions for the language to be gradually lost in the areas of contact with the Romance languages. In the sixteenth century, Basque was being lost in Araba, in the Encartaciones and south of Lizarra/Estella. The regression was becoming worrisome in the eighteenth century and alarming in the nineteenth century. The greater part of Navarra, including Iruñea, no longer spoke Basque, as had occurred earlier in Araba. Worse still, there seemed to be no way to stop the process. The subordinate status of Basque as opposed to the official languages was compounded by increasingly grievous prohibitions. In the seventeenth century it was already forbidden to teach or print books in Basque. The massive arrival of alien population to Bilbao and Bizkaia's mining area in the late nineteenth century accelerated the loss of the language in the capital of the province of Bizkaia.

There was a reaction, of course. The Academy of the Language (Euskaltzaindia) was founded, as well as the first *ikastolak* (schools where the teaching was in Basque). Literature written in Basque was encouraged, and when the first Basque government came to power in 1936-1937, the Basque language was finally used in government. However, Franco's dictatorship

Meeting of Euskalzaindia with Basque writers. The year 1927. Above, from left to right, Orixe, Jean Elissalde, Seber Altube, Julio Urquijo and Ramon Olabide. Seated, Juan Bautista Eguzkitza, Bonifacio de Echegaray, Resurrección María Azkue and Georges Lacombe.

Celebration of Olentzero, the Basque Christmas, by girls and boys in the ikastola in Ordizia (Gipuzkoa). 1969.

Party to celebrate the end of Bai Euskarari campaign (1978). Around 40,000 people gathered in the San Mamés soccer stadium.

(1937-1975) cut the process short and persecuted the language ferociously because they considered that Spaniards should speak Spanish. The French Jacobin state born of the Revolution had the same idea for France: knowledge of the French language was imposed, although it did not succeed in spreading to the rural area of the three Basque provinces governed by the French until the twentieth century.

In the mid 1950s, the situation was critical. In the north, French was taught in the schools and used by for government and the military service until it was spoken in everywhere, even within the families, its last bastion. In the four peninsular provinces, speaking Basque was persecuted harshly. That, combined with the massive arrival of alien people, accelerated the regression of the Basque language that had started several centuries earlier. Euskera was weakened in Bizkaia, in all the urban areas of the country, and in Pyrenean Navarre.

At the worst possible time, when the flame threatened to splutter out, a popular reaction broke out. Clandestine *ikastolak* were set up, followed by *gau-eskolak* (night schools to teach the language to adults); written literature, music in Basque and the *bertsolariak* (singers of musical verse) resurfaced. The movement spread throughout the country in the 60s and 70s. Euskaltzaindia (the Basque Academy of the Language) gave the go-ahead to a standard unified Basque (euskera batúa) that allowed the language to be adapted to contemporary needs (communication, culture, education, administration etc.). The death of the dictator and the constitution of the first Basque institutions (municipalities, provincial councils and the Basque and Navarrean governments) led to Basque being spoken in the official spheres for the first time: in state schools and the universities, and in the government in general. Basque was also spoken in the media, especially with the important step of creating a public broadcasting company: EiTB.

It is true that popular movements have always been ahead of the institutions, even those that have been elected democratically. Such is the case of the massive popular festivals that are held every year in order to raise funds for the *ikastolas*. The festivals are called in Gipuzkoa are called Kilometroak; in Bizkaia, Ibilaldia; in Araba, Araba Euskaraz; in Nafarroa, Nafarroa Oinez, and in Ipar Euska Herria, Herri Urrats. Also, every two years, a surprising two-week relay race carries a message in defence of the Basque language throughout the Basque Country. It is the Korrika, in which people of any age, condition and ideology participate in support of the Basque language.

Other key elements are also the product of popular initiatives, such as the press in Basque, which includes the only daily newspaper published in Basque (*Berria*, the successor of *Euskaldunon Egunkaria*); many local and regional magazines and publications; radio stations; Udako Euskal Unibertsitatea (the Basque Summer University) and several publishing houses.

Currently, the status of Euskera differs according to the territories in which it is used. It is

EGUNA

PAXISTEN EGAZKIÑAK

Gernika, euzkotaren uri maitea, birindu nai izan dabe zearo

Aritza zutik gelditu da, ordea, ondamendi oretan. Zutikago euzkotaren gogoa, baña.

Guda oñetako agiriak

GABEKO IZPARRAK

EUZKADI

Donosti Buru Batsafo

Gure irakurlei

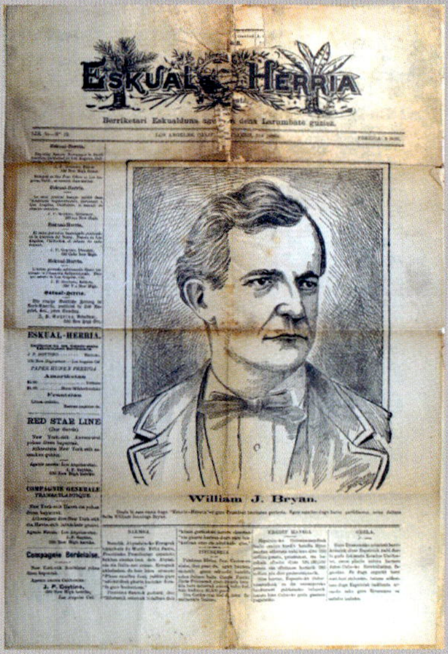
ESKUAL HERRIA

William J. Bryan.

LE NUMERO : 5 CENTIMES

ESKUALDUNA

JOURNAL BASQUE-FRANÇAIS HEBDOMADAIRE

Gerla Haste - Biba Frantzia!

HERRIALDE AUZOAK GURE ALDE

BERRIAK

Three covers of publications in Basque: Eguna (Bilbao, daily, 1937), Eskual Herria (California, weekly, 1893-1897) and Eskualduna (Baiona, bilingual weekly, 1887-1944).

the official language, along with Spanish, in Bizkaia, Gipuzkoa, Araba and north of Navarre; has some rights recognized in part of the middle area Navarre; and lacks any legal protection in the rest of the autonomous region of Navarre and the three Basque provinces inland. The result is that while a child in Baztan (Navarre) or Gernika (Bizkaia) has no problem in studying Basque in the local public school, the language is forbidden to schoolchildren in the southern half of Navarre and all of Ipar Euskal Herria. It is true, however, that there are bilingual public schools in the north. Even so, it is difficult to speak Basque in everyday life, even in the more Basque-speaking towns of the area where the language is official. Health care in the Basque language is not guaranteed, for instance; not even for small children who have not yet learned Spanish.

The degree of fluency in the language also varies, depending on the region and by age. In general, the generations directly affected by Franco's dictatorship have the lowest proportion of *euskaldunak* (speakers of Basque). On the contrary, most of those who are under age 25 know the language.

Currently, all Basque speakers are bilingual, speaking another language, especially Spanish or French, as well as their own. The province with more *euskaldunak* is Gipuzkoa (50%), followed by Bizkaia (25 %), Ipar Euskal Herria (21 %, although both Zuberoa and Nafarroa Beherea are above 50%), Araba (16%) and Nafarroa (12%). That comes to more than 700,000 people, to which we could add another 100,000 who are learning to speak the language or can understand it.

More people understand Basque than those who speak it. This is partly due to statistics, because, since all those who speak Basque are bilingual, they switch to Spanish or French in the presence of anyone who does not understand Basque. In any case, the many years of contempt for the language have also taken a toll. In much of the country, the first word spoken upon meeting someone new will never be in Basque.

The future of the language is uncertain. On the one hand, there is a broad social consensus to promote Basque, linguistic activism is dynamic and instruments to preserve the language are being implemented in much of the country. In areas where the language is official (Bizkaia, Gipuzkoa, Araba and north of Nafarroa), the majority of schoolchildren - three out of every four - study in Basque. On the other hand, the language still takes second place in the fields where its use has not been regulated, such as the world of work, health, and on the streets of a large part of the country's biggest cities. In addition, the Basque language faces competition from powerful languages such as French or Spanish, in which all Basques are proficient, in addition to the emerging importance of knowing English. Furthermore, the lack of support or, directly, the obstacles imposed by the various administrations are slowing down the recovery or favouring the loss of the language. Once Basque has become a minority language, prohibiting it will no longer be necessary; it will be sufficient to deny it strong support. This is obvious in Navarre/Nafarroa, whose government has openly discouraged the recovery of the language in recent years. The most delicate situation has been detected in Soule/Zuberoa, where the older generations are Basque-speaking but only a very small minority of young people knows the language. There the ancestral chain has been broken. The struggle of the Basques to remain euskaldunak will continue, at least for a few generations more.

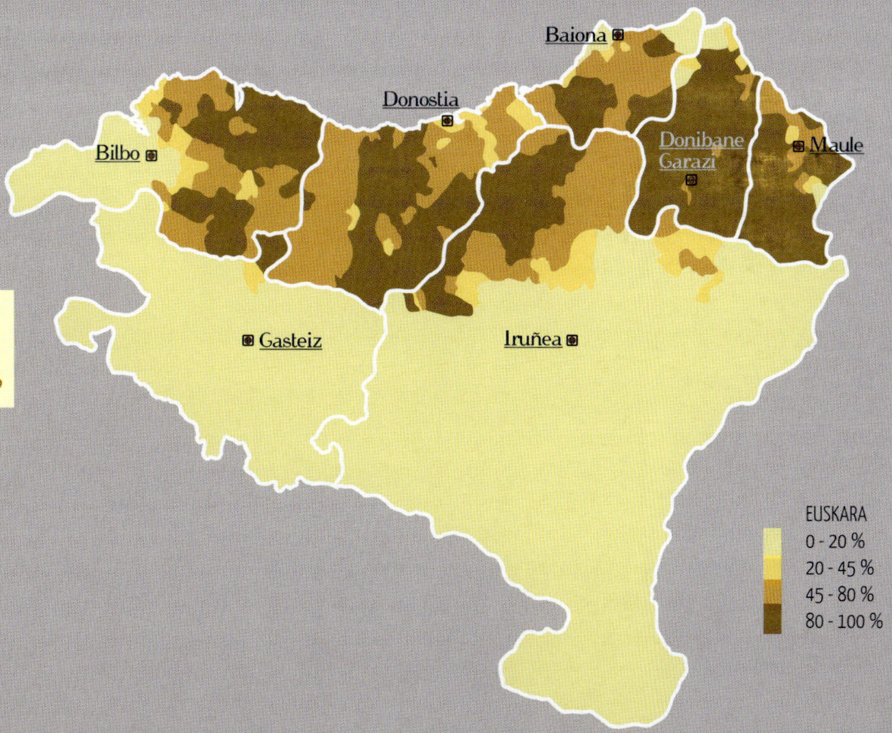

Density of the Basque language by municipalities

Basque is the language of most of the population in the eastern half of Bizkaia, most of Gipuzkoa, northwest Navarre and the inland area of the French Basque Country/Ipar Euskal Herria. However, the customs differ, for Basque is becoming more widespread in Bizkaia, Gipuzkoa, Araba and part of Navarre, whereas north of the Pyrenees the transfer to the next generation seems to be broken.

Source: Fourth Sociolinguistic Survey (2006).

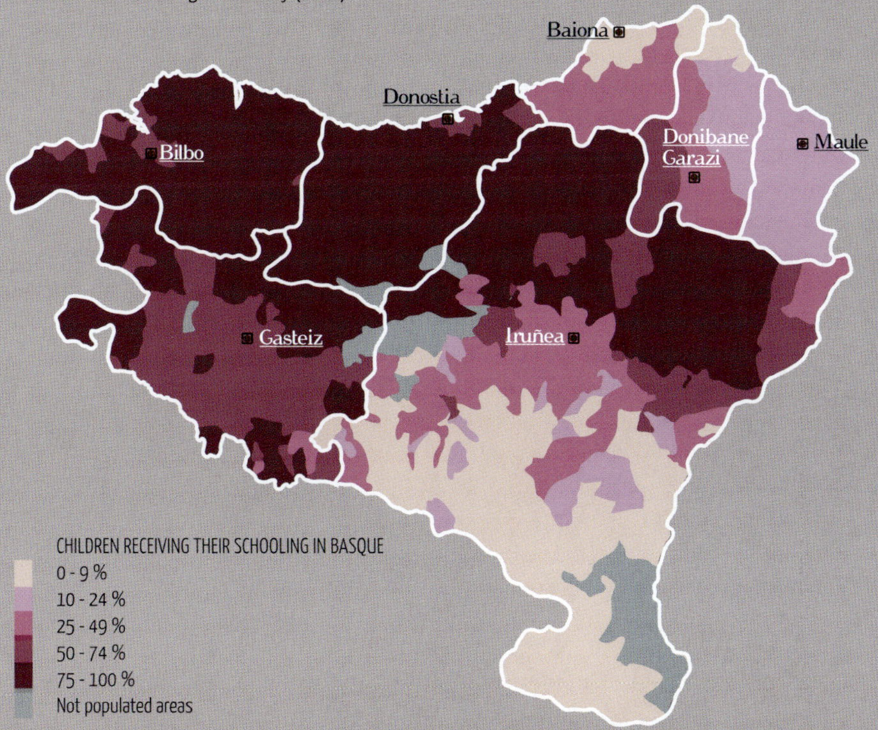

Map of enrolment in the basque language by municipalities

Mothers, fathers, teachers and a few institutions have made an effort in the last 30 years to promote learning in the Basque language. Teaching in most of the Basque Country is now in Basque, and the younger generations are now fluent. The situation in the most of Navarre and the French Basque Country/Ipar Euskal Herria is still difficult, however.

Source: Euskara Kultur Elkargoa.

Zangoza. Nafarroa Oinez.

Galdakao. Ibilaldia.

Kilometroak.

in favour of Basque

Biarritz. Korrika.

Gasteiz. Korrika.

Senpere. Herri Urrats.

Laudio. Araba Euskaraz.

Korrika.

WRITTEN LITERATURE:
a difficult road ahead

In comparison to Spanish and French, literature written in the Basque language was late and of little significance, at least until the end of the twentieth century. In this regard, its development has not been very different from people in similar circumstances. Most of the literature has been limited to religious themes and has had to cope with problems such as the absence of a unified literary language and the lack of literate readers. Despite this, it has generated a legacy that is interesting, although modest. Currently, around 1,500 books written in Basque are published every year, of which 15% correspond to fiction; a relevant figure, considering the potential market.

Compared to the literature in the adjacent languages (currently French and Spanish, Occitan and Arabic in the Middle Ages), Basque lags far behind. If, on the contrary, we take into consideration the historical conditions in which the language has developed and the manner in which it has been relegated and even persecuted, Basque is surprisingly resilient. The amount of oral literature in Basque is unexpectedly large, however.

Many Basques have written great works in other languages, especially Spanish and French. This is the case of Miguel de Unamuno, Pio Baroja and, more recently, Luis Martín-

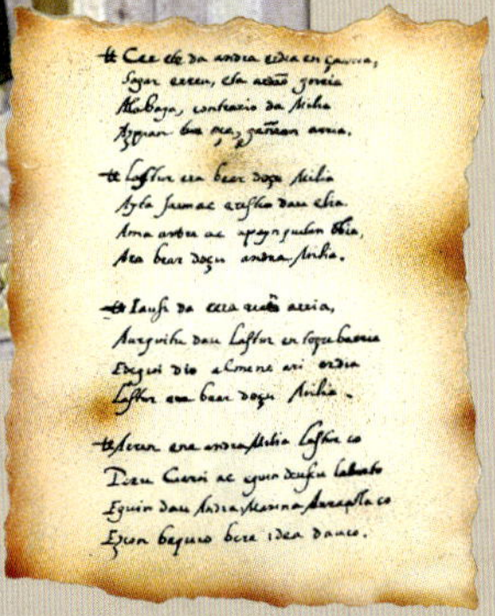

A medieval engraving depicting a poetess. Beside her, lyrics of a 15th funeral song (eresi) by Milia Lasturkoa.

Santos and Gabriel Celaya. Many modern Basque authors write in French or Spanish, like Marie Darrieussecq, Toti Martínez de Lezea, Miguel Sanchez Ostiz and Espido Freire.

Covers of the first books published in Basque: Linguae Vasconum Primitiae (1545) and the New Testament, translated by Leizarraga (1572).

The first Basque literature had a female voice

Logically, it is conceivable that there were older literary compositions, but there are no known works prior to the fourteenth century. The clan wars in that century and the next devastated the country and left a trail of lyrical compositions. Although they belonged to the oral tradition, the few that have survived were preserved in texts published in the sixteenth century or collected by folklorists from the lips of the populace in the early nineteenth century.

The Fuero Viejo (Old Law) of Bizkaia (1453) cites a few women called *profazadas* who "sing verses and songs by way of libel and slander". The *profazadas*' songs were funeral dirges known as *eresiak*, which were sung at burials. Many were a tribute to those who were killed in the clan wars. There are several fragments of ballads that recreate moments of great significance in that conflict, such as the burning of Arrasate (1448). The most important ballad of all is the *Bereterretxeren kantoria*, an anonymous fifteenth century poem that recounts the tragic death of a popular youth from Soule who died a tragic death at the hands of the Lord of Maule.

The Basque language goes to press

In the sixteenth century, while the national languages of the western monarchies were replacing Latin and joined their fortunes to those of their states, the Basque language appeared in written literature without a state to be linked to and without creating a stir. At first then language was included in the works of others, as in the song of Perucho in the third part of the Celestina (1536) or the Basque text reproduced in Pantagruel, by François Rabelais (1542). Later, Basque titles were printed.

The first book published in Basque language, *Linguae vasconum Primitiae*, was the work of Bernat Etxepare (1545), a priest from Lower Navarre. It contained a handful of poems on religious themes and romantic love. As he announced in the title, the author was aware that he was starting a new era for the Basque language, which was considered barbaric and irreducible to writing because it did not derive from Latin.

The work we describe next is said to be the only one in the literature written in Basque that was sponsored by a head of state. Queen Juana de Albret tried to extend Protestantism in the lands under her rule, which included Nafarroa Beherea. Under her aegis *Iesus Christ Gure Iaunaren Testamentu Berria*, the first Basque version of the New Testament, was printed in 1572 . The translation was directed by Joanes Leizarraga, a priest in Beskoitze, near Bayonne. He has gone down in history for his effort to create a unified literary language and for making Basque one of the languages in which the Bible could be read, precisely at the time most European languages were taking the same step. For once, the Basques were no too late.

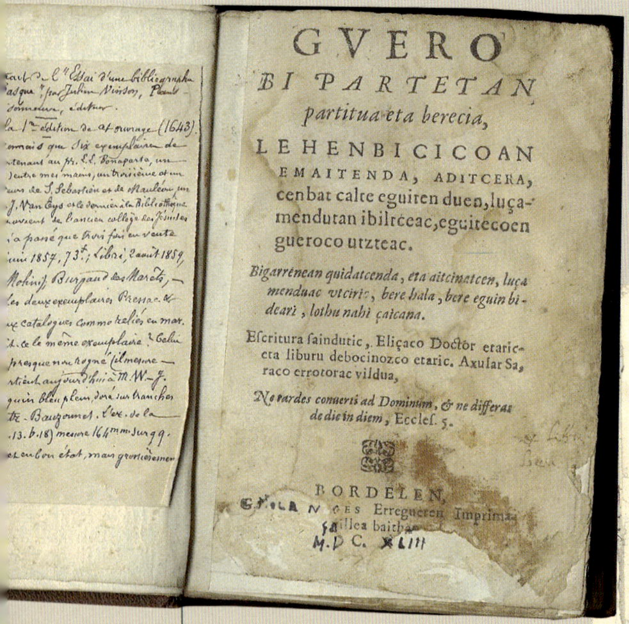

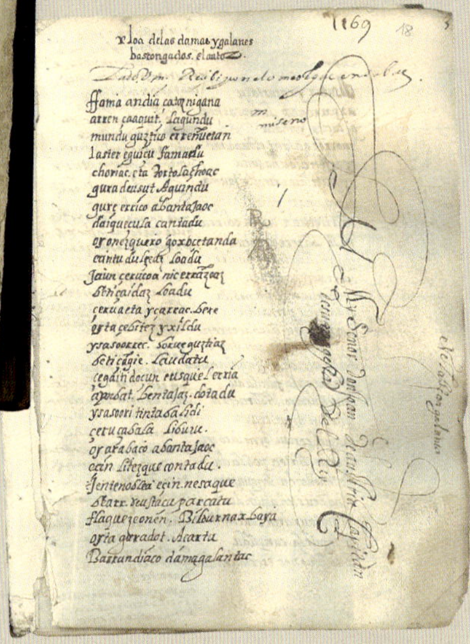

First edition of Gero, the classic work by Axular. Beside it, the manuscript of Juan Perez de Lazarraga, from Alava.

A suspect break

Unfortunately, the Basque language's début in the press had little continuity. As far as we know, only four works went to press in all of the sixteenth century: the work written by Etxepare and three by Leizarraga). To these we should add two bilingual catechisms (published in Bilbao and Lizarra) and a collection of proverbs. But there were more to come. Numerous traces attest to this, especially poems that sometimes denote an aristocratic origin. Without doubt, the most important work, unknown until 2004, is the manuscript of Juan Perez de Alava Lazarraga, which includes part of a pastoral novel, and religious and secular poems on several topics.

The unexpected finding of the manuscript of Lazarraga and the suspicion that other works may have existed have led some scholars to argue that there was a tradition of writing literature in Basque among the literate classes until the end of the sixteenth century. If so, the effort only had continuity in the part of the country that belonged to the French crown. In the four peninsular provinces, the break is obvious: in the next 200 years only a handful of bilingual religious works were published, in Basque and Spanish, as if the authorities did not trust texts that were written solely in the impenetrable barbarian language.

The school in Sara

North of the river Bidasoa, the dynamic province of Lapurdi, with a booming maritime economy, provided moments of grandeur for Basque literature. In 1617, the first book in original prose written entirely in Basque was published. It was a prayer book written by Materre, and is sparked a relatively large production of spiritual works by authors such as Joanes Haranburu, Joanes Etxeberri and, above all, Pedro Agerre, alias *Axular*. They were all ecclesiastics who lived between Sara, Donibane Lohizune and Ziburu, so they were known as the *Sarako Eskola* (the Sara school).

The main figure of the group was *Axular*, a priest from Navarre who served as parish priest in Sara. His work ascetic *Gero* (1643) is regarded as the great classic of the Basque literature, both for its aesthetic beauty as for its masterful use of language.

Preachers come into action

The Basque literary production in Ipar Euskal Herria maintained its supremacy throughout the seventeenth century and was extended to the eighteenth century. However, in the latter century the initiative was going to Gipuzkoa, where the Jesuit Manuel de Larramendi took over. Despite the fact that he almost always wrote in Spanish, he successfully stirred up the quiet waters of Basque culture with his effort to raise awareness and his work *El Imposible Vencido* (The Impossible Achieved), the significant title under which the first Basque grammar was published. By then, Basque was comparable to the most advanced languages.

Larramendi's thesis spread throughout the country. There were those who admired its linguistic purity and neologisms. The true greatness of the work by the Jesuit from Andoain was the defence of the language, his attempt to restore its prestige, and his desire to extend it to all areas of life. Larramendi's call to awareness found an echo among the preacher friars. Augustine Kardaberaz and Sebastian Mendiburu wrote numerous works, the majority, of course, with a religious content, although there was also some rhetoric -*Euskararen Berri Onak*, by Kardaberaz (1761) - and criticism of the "lewd" popular dances, from Mendiburu.

In any case, most of eighteenth century Basque literature, as in previous centuries, was in lyric genre. The new centralist state of the Spanish branch of the Bourbon monarchs banned the publishing of works in Basque on several occasions.

Above, a friar preaching from a pulpit. Below, works by Kardaberaz, Mendiburu and Larramendi.

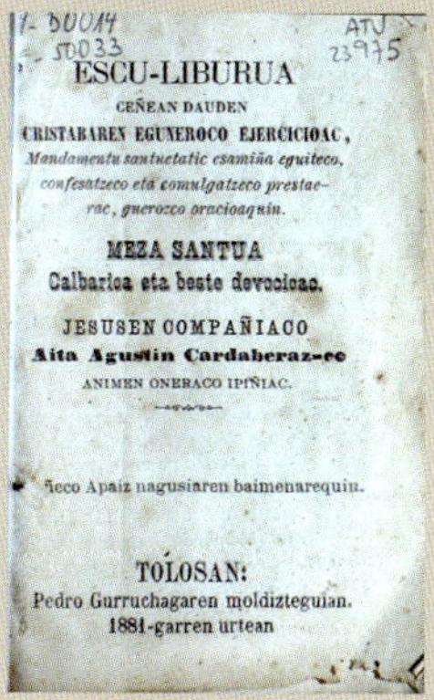

ESCU-LIBURUA
CEÑEAN DAUDEN
CRISTABAREN EGUNEROCO EJERCICIOAC,
Mandamentu santuetatic esamiña eguiteco, confesatzeco eta comulgatzeco prestaerac, guerozco oracioaquin.
MEZA SANTUA
Calbarioa eta beste devocioac.
JESUSEN COMPAÑIACO
Aita Agustin Cardaberaz-ec
ANIMEN ONERACO IPIÑIAC.
...eco Apaiz nagusiaren baimenarequin.
TOLOSAN:
Pedro Gurruchagaren moldizteguian.
1881-garren urtean

JESUS·EN
COMPAÑIACO
A. SEBASTIAN MENDIBURUC
euscaraz eracusten duen
JESUS-EN BIHOTZA-REN
Devocioa.
Behar bezala. Bi-garren aldian.
Iruñean. Pedro Joseph Ezquerro, Libruguillea-ren echean, 1751, Urtean

DICCIONARIO
TRILINGUE
DEL
CASTELLANO,
BASCUENCE,
Y LATIN.
TOMO PRIMERO.
SU AUTOR
EL PADRE MANUEL DE LARRA...
de la Compañia de Jesus.
DEDICADO
A LA MUI NOBLE,
Y MUI LEAL PROVINCIA
DE GUIPUZCOA.
AÑO 1745.
CON PRIVILEGIO EN SAN SEBASTIAN:

The stormy Romantic era

As the nineteenth century progressed, the Basque language was gradually being lost in peninsular Euskal Herria and in the social life of the country. The elites marked distances with the people, and instead of learning other languages, as they had until then, they stopped speaking their own. Ignorance became a sign of distinction.

In other fields, the language was making progress. The nineteenth century saw the birth of folklore and the concern for collecting a disappearing oral culture from the mouths of the people. In Euskal Herria a valuable part of Basque oral literature was saved from being lost. In addition to collecting songs, stories and beliefs, authors such as Francisque Michel or

Drawing by Joan Ignazio Iztueta, folklorist and poet. His Kontzesiri have been handed down to the present by word of mouth.

José Manterola published them, which led to their dissemination.

The romantic spirit the prompted the collection of folklore could also be felt in many popular poems, such as *Kontxesiri*, by Joan Ignazio Iztueta; *Aire delizius hontan* by the poet from Soule, Pierre Topet, alias Etxabun; in the texts of the visionary Agosti Xaho; and in the immortal songs of Jose Maria Iparragirre, author of the *Gernikako Arbola*". In the meantime, the religious literary tradition increased and was reinforced with the settlement of a remarkable group that wrote in the Biscayan dialect, led by Juan Antonio Mogel. Curiously, his best work, *Peru Abarka*, is not religious but a fictional prose narrative, in the form of a dialogue.

In the course of the nineteenth century, Basque made peace with the printing press. The first bilingual magazines or exclusively in Basque (after the second Carlist War) were printed in Euskal Herria (*Euskalzale*) and in the diaspora (*Eskual Herria* in California). More important were the many pamphlets printed with verses. The *bertsolariak*, the improvisers of verses, found that the pamphlets were a source of income and a way disseminating their works. The poets with the most talent became renowned in the wake of the pamphlets. Indalecio Bizkarrondo, alias *Bilintx*, a writer from San Sebastián, for example, belongs by right to the above-mentioned group of romantic authors.

Despite the social decline of the language, the Carlist wars, the suppression of the Fueros and the advance of industrialization appeared about to put an end to rural life in the Basque Country, movements were also under way to lay foundations for the future. One example was the brainchild of Soule-born Anton Abbadia, who started the *Lore Jokoak* (floral games) as lyric contest in 1853. Jean Baptiste Etxahun, Gratian Adema Zaldubi and Joanes Oxalde were the most distinguished winners. The romantic sentiment of renewal of the language and Basque identity had other literary expressions. At that time, the theater in Basque experienced a period of splendour, with such authors as Marcelino Soroa.

New roads

Basque nationalism emerged in the late 19th century, given a new impetus for the recovery and use of the Basque language. The effort to renew and standardise the Basque language and literature came under the name of *Euskal Pizkundea* and lasted until 1936, when it was cut short by the fascist revolt. The modest journalistic and literary activity in Basque (like *Zeruko Argia*, 1917 and *Argia*, 1921), the contests and, of course, a source of ecclesiastics provided new names that opened up unprecedented roads for Basque culture.

Poetry remained the most widespread form of literature in the country. Julen Urkiza has registered more than 16,000 poetic compositions published in magazines between 1900 and 1937, which gives an idea of poetry's popularity. In the early twentieth century, the first groups of women (Sorne Unzueta, Errose Bustintza and Katalina Eleizegi, to name a few) made their appearance on the Basque literary scene for the first time since the sixteenth century.

Eusko Olerki Eguna (Day of Basque Poetry) held in Errenteria in 1930. On the right, poet Claudio Sagarzazu reads his poetry during the Basque festivals in Hondarribia (1925). Below, poets Lizardi and Orixe (on the right) in a tribute to writer Bittor Garitaonaindia (1932).

In the meantime, the narrative was finally making progress. The first novel written in the Basque language was a historical-romantic work, *Auñemendiko Lorea* (1898), by Txomin Agirre, which paved the way for milestones like *Garoa* (1906) and *Kresala* (1912), depicting local everyday life and customs. Other authors continued in the same vein: versatile Resurrection María Azkue, Jean Barbier, Pierre Lhande, José Manuel Etxeita, and many others.

Short stories also saw a remarkable development. Authors Jean Etxepare, Enrike Zubiri Manezaundi and Ebaristo Bustintza, alias *Kirikiño*, achieved great renown with their chronicles. The theatre experienced one of its moments of splendour, with a large production centered in Donostia around authors of the importance of Toribio Altzaga and Abelin Barriola.

A generation known as the *Olerkariak* (poets) flourished in the third decade of the twentieth century under the lead of José Ariztimuño, alias *Aitzol*. The two maximum figures in the group, Xabier Lizardi and Esteban Urkiaga, *Lauaxeta*, and *Aitzol*, died in 1935-1937 at the height of their youth. *Lauaxeta* and *Aitzol* were executed by the Francoists. Their poetry was absolutely contemporary poetry, daring in both style and language. Works such as *Biotz Begietan* (1932), by Lizardi, a master of synthesis and a minstrel of nature; and *Arrats Beran* (1935), by *Lauaxeta*, which combines classicism, popular literature and avant-garde, led the way for Basque poetry toward thematic and aesthetic maturity.

The third prominent poet of the *Olerkariak* group was Nikolas Ormaetxea, *Orixe*. In exile, first, and then upon his return in 1954, he served as a link between his generation and the groups that sought to renew the Basque language and literature insofar as Franco's dictatorship allowed.

Gabriel Aresti at the Arrate cross with family and friends.

Exile and regeneration

The Spanish civil war and World War II (1936-1945) proved devastating for Basque literature. At first it was reconstructed on another continent, in America, to which many of the exiles fled. Buenos Aires, with the publishing house Ekin, and Guatemala, with the magazine *Euzko Gogoa*, became beacons of hope. Authors like *Orixe*, Martin Ugalde, Telesforo Monzón and Jokin Zaitegi published their works from the exile in America.

Arantzazu (1949), a collection of poems by the Franciscan Salbatore Mitxelena was the first major work published in Hego Euskal Herria after the war. It got passed the censorship due to its obvious religious overtones. But the times were beginning to change. On the one hand, Franco's dictatorship was finding it increasingly difficult to maintain an absolute prohibition of Basque; and on the other, Ipar Euskal Herria began to accept some of the exiles again, and literary activity picked up again. More importantly, the country was changing: industrialization progressed and with it, the urban way of life. Migrants from other regions of Spain arrived en masse and a new political force, ETA, posed a more active resistance.

Society was becoming more dynamic, as reflected in the appearance of publications, some bilingual, like *Egan* (since 1954) and others entirely in Basque, like *Karmel* (1950), *Anaitasuna* (1953) *Jakin* (1956) and *Argia* (1963). In addition, the publishing house *Itxaropena* start a collection of titles in the Basque language. So modest an infrastructure began to bear fruit. A group of writers (Federico Krutwig, Gabriel Aresti, Juan San Martín, José Luis Alvarez Enparantza, alias *Txillardegi*, and Jon Mirande) gathered around Egan, made a definitive break with the traditionalist legacy and brought modernity to the Basque culture. The most prominent literary figures were Aresti, at the summit of Basque social poetry thanks to works such as *Harri Herri* eta (1964); *Txillardegi*, whose first novel, *Leturiaren egunkari ezkutua* (1957), was along clearly existentialist lines; and Jon Mirande, an atypical author from Soule who wrote vitalist poetry and the novel *Haur Besoetakoa* (1970), a variant of Lolita written by someone who had never read Nabokov's work.

Social poetry, existentialism, romantic irrationalism ... despite the constraints of the dictatorship, Basque literature was being opened up to modernity. Two more significant steps were taken in the 60s. One was the development of *euskera batua* (unified Basque), the standard required for modern activities. The other was the Durango Book Fair, dedicated to basque works, which opened for the first time in 1965. Since then it plays a critical role in the Basque Country's publishing world.

Franciscan friar Salbatore Mitxelena published the first important work in Basque in Hego Euskal Herria since the Spanish Civil War. His book of poems, Arantzazu, opened a road that had been forbidden until then.

The novel Soinujolearen semea (2003) is the most widely translated work in Basque literature.

Toward standardisation

Although poetry continued to generate works of great impact, narrative began to gain importance. Authors Anjel Lertxundi, Arantxa Urretabizkaia and Ramon Saizarbitoria published novels as relevant as *Egunero hasten Delako* (1969), *Ajea du Urturik* (1971) and *Zergatik Panpox* (1979). The country was stirring with a yearning to regain freedom and the Basque language on the wave of creativity unleashed after forty years of dictatorship. When Franco died in 1975, Basque began to be spoken in the administration, progress was made education, and aids were given to publishing. All this was done with great difficulty, however, because the situation of the Basque language had become critical. Since then the country has created a modest Basque literary system with a network of publishers, bookshops, critics, translators, magazines and, above all, writers and readers. Publishers of humble origins, almost linked to the underground, such as Erein (1976) and Elkar (1972), have become points of reference by setting up a group comprising several publishers, a distributor and bookshops. More recent publishing houses are Susa, Pamiela, Maiatz, Txalaparta and Igela. They have published contemporary Basque literature as well as translations of a large part of the world classics and some of the latest international works.

Basque literature has grown significantly since 1975. Most of the works are narrative, although short stories are also published, in some periods more than the novel. The avant-garde literary magazines *Ustela* and *Pott* published the next wave of great authors who consolidated modern literature with their attractive, high quality works. Bernardo Atxaga, the writer most awarded and translated, has marked an epoch with works such as *Etiopia* (poetry, 1978) and the novels *Obabakoak*

Itxaro Borda.

Txillardegi.

Karmele Jaio.

Ramon Saizarbitoria.

Joseba Sarrionandia.

Koldo Izagirre.

Aingeru Epaltza.

Bernardo Atxaga and Xabier Lete.

Uxue Alberdi.

(1988), *Soinujolearen Semea* (2003) and *Zazpi etxe Frantzian* (2009). Koldo Izagirre also writes poetry and novels, with such brilliant results as *Balizko erroten erresuma* (poetry, 1989), *Euzkadi merezi zuten* (novel, 1985) and *Sua nahi, Mr. Churchill?* (tales, 2005). Last but not least, Joseba Sarrionandia has become a point of reference for his suggestive style in poetry (*Izuen gordelekuetan barrena*, 1981), the short story (*Narrazioak*, 1983, was a milestone), the novel (*Lagun Izoztua*, 2001) and the essay.

The next literary generation successfully addressed a wide variety of themes and styles. Aingeru Epaltza, for example, has produced historical novels (three works on the conquest of Nafarroa) and detective novels (*Rock and Roll*, 2000), among other genres. Jon Alonso, Pako Aristi, Itxaro Borda, Edorta Jimenez, Miren Agur Meabe, Xabier Mendiguren and Xabier Montoia are some of the most outstanding authors. After them came a new generation, dubbed *Lubaki Band*, in the 90s. Of those young authors, the most recognized literary career was forged by Harkaitz Cano, author of novels of great impact: *Belarraren Ahoa* (2004) and *Twist* (2011). Children's literature has also produced many important works. One of the most recognised authors is Mariasun Landa, who has seen her works translated into many languages. New names are constantly emerging in the publishing world (Uxue Alberdi, Eider Rodriguez...); young authors like Karmele Jaio and Kirmen Uribe, who have had highly interesting careers.

ORAL LITERATURE,
a treasure by word of mouth

There are many cultures that have preserved their literary heritage orally. Banned from the printing press until the nineteenth century, the Basque language survived as a rich source of oral literature in the form of songs, stories, legends, ballads, proverbs, improvised verses and popular theatre.

Folk songs and ballads

The *kopla zaharrak* (ancient folk songs) have served as the lyrical moulds for the main social events of the rural Basque life. Christmas, New Year and Santa Agueda have witnessed the rites of passage in which folk songs play a key role. Despite their antiquity, the popular songs have adapted to changing fashions. Sometimes they were embedded in ballads, as in the case of the immortal *Bereterretxeren Kantoria*. They also became the habitual pattern for the lyrics of the songs sung to the tune of the *trikitixa* or diatonic accordion.

Basque ballads have been divided into three groups, depending on their content, trends and time. The oldest ballads (fifteenth and sixteenth centuries), like *Beotibarko Gudua*, were about the clan wars. Epic-lyrical ballads were sung in the seventeenth century. Despite their undertones of nobility, they were not chronicles of a period but invented arguments, as in *Brodatzen ari nintzen*. Love songs in the form of dialogue were the dominant theme in the eighteenth century, as in the famous *Maitia nun zira?*

Bertsolaris Txirrita, Olegario and Gaztelu in Arrate (Eibar, 1915). On the right, Xalbador in the bertsolaris championship (Donostia, 1967).

More than 13,000 people filled the Bilbao Exhibition Centre in Barakaldo to watch the finals of the Euskal Herria bertsolaris championship (2013).

Bertsolaris, words as a sport

There was a time, apparently in the second third of the nineteenth century, in which this type of literary production went out of fashion. It was replaced in some areas by *bertso berriak* (new verses, as opposed to the old ones). These were the compositions of the *bertsolariak* (improvisers of verses) which, conveniently copied and printed, began to be sold in pamphlets. Although the tradition of improvising verses is immemorial, it seems that the *bertsolaris* were limited to challenging each other in the taverns and cider houses until they began to perform in public squares at the beginning of the nineteenth century. In 1801, thousands of people gathered in Villabona to witness the challenge between Zabala and Txabolategi.

The peddling of verses had supplanted traditional ballads and the tradition of improvising verses in some areas, particularly in Gipuzkoa, although they were maintained Bizkaia and Zuberoa. A new model emerged in their place, the bertsolari, dissociated from the symbolic universe that governed folk songs and able to assemble long verses on a variety of topics. The *bertsolari* constructed their verses backwards, by thinking of the last sentence first and going on from there.

Although there were *bertsolaris* in every province, the epicentre seems to have developed around the culture of cider, in the valleys of the rivers Urumea and Oria. That is where the classical *bertsolari* came from, including Frantzisko Petrirena *Xenpelar*, Pedro José Elizegi *Pello Errota*, and Pello Mari Otaño. With the exception of the latter, due to his weak voice, they all combined the improvisation of verses in squares and taverns with the publication of pamphlets of *bertso berriak*.

The most outstanding of the next generation of *bertsolari* was José Manuel Lujanbio, *Txirrita* (1860-1936), perhaps the first *bertsolari* to attain fame throughout the Basque regions. A archetypical bertsolari, mischievous, unmarried and a great merrymaker, *Txirrita* boasted an exceptional gift for the dialectical duels held in the cider houses and, at the same time, he had the ability of dealing with the thornier issues of current interest with passion and common sense.

Txirrita took part in Euskal Herria's first *bertsolari* championship, which was sponsored by José Ariztimuno *Aitzol* and held in Donostia in 1935. *Txirrita* did not win on that occasion, although he did in 1936. The first competition was won by Inazio Eizmendi *Basarri*, a young man who embodied the new generation. Sadly, that generation of *bertsolari* was buried on the battlefield or silenced by the Francoist repression. *Basarri* and Manuel Olaizola *Uztapide*, kept the flame alive until the next reinforcement by Manuel Lasarte, Jon Azpillaga, Jon Lopategi and the Enbeita family. The verses of Fernando Aire *Xalbador*, the shepherd from Urepele endowed with a breathtaking lyrical vein still resonate in Ipar Euskal Herria.

After the long silence imposed by Franco, the improvisation of verses was in a difficult position, closely associated with the rural world in a society that was urban and mostly not Basque-speaking. In this impasse, some contributions proved decisive. On the one hand, there was the transcendental renewal introduced by Xabier Amuriza at the formal level (metaphors, melodies and metric) and linguistic level. He was the first to improvise in *Euskera batua*, the unified Basque language established a few years earlier. On the other hand, there was the decision to create *bertso eskolak*, schools that might be formed the *bertsolaris* of the future. The schools produced young generation of bertsolari, like Jon Sarasua and Xabier Perez *Euzkitze*, in the 80s. Currently most of the new *bertsolaris* come from the *bertso eskolak*.

Amuriza won the *bertsolari* championships in 1980 and 1982. The impulse he gave to the improvisation of verses has not stopped since then. *Bertsolaritza* has grown to become a mass phenomenon in a society that is clearly urban. The finals of the Euskal Herria championship filled the Anoeta velodrome (8,000 people) until they were moved to the BEC (Bilbao Exhibition Centre) in Barakaldo, which can seat 13,000 people. Apart from the live performances, the competitions are highly popular on television, radio programs and the press. Champion *bertsolaris* like Andoni Egaña, Maialen Lujanbio and Amets Arzallus enjoyed great prestige in the Basque cultural panorama.

Image of the pastoral Akitaniako Alienor, performed in Maule in 2014.

Popular theatre: the pastorals

Pastorals are undoubtedly the country's most singular form of popular theatre. They are only performed in Soule/Zuberoa. Scholars believe that the pastorals came to this corner of the country from the mystères or medieval mystery plays, although there is no record of when they made their appearance or why they were never performed in the rest of the Basque Country. The oldest record of a pastoral goes back to 1634, when *Jundane Jakobe Handiaren Trajeria* was performed in Atharratze/Tardets-Sorholus.

In general, the Soule pastorals tell the story of a character considered to be of special interest, normally saints, biblical characters and great French heroes. In the mid-twentieth century, Pierre Bordazaharre *Etxahun-Iruri* shifted the focus to the history of Euskal Herria, in his main characters (*Zumalakarregi*, 1989) and relevant events (*Euskaldunak Ibañetan*, 1954; *Xiberoko makia*, 2001).

The pastorals reflect a Manichaean duality, with good characters (*khirixtiak*, Christians) and bad (*turkak*, Turks). Normally the message is delivered before the play starts and summarized at the end (*azken pheredikia*). The characters sing their verses, interspersing the recitals with dance steps. Although the pastorals were once performed in churches, they have been staged in the open air for a long time. There are usually two performances of each play, on two consecutive Sundays. Each year a different town in Zuberoa is responsible for the play and the townspeople take care of the preparations, rehearsals, production and performance.

BASQUE MYTHOLOGY, an amazing universe

No written record of the ancient religion of the Basques has been preserved. There is no legacy for posterity, sacred scriptures, temples or tombs of high priests. If that were not enough, for more than a thousand years Christianity has been the dominant creed in a country that has suffered appalling witch hunts (sixteenth and seventeenth centuries). Nonetheless, we know a lot about the old religion. How is this possible? Thanks to a rich oral literature and the deep roots of some atavistic beliefs. Legends, superstitions and rituals that still show traces of ancient goddesses and fantastic beings have been passed down through generations. Everything seems to

indicate that the old religion of the Basques lasted, in part, until recent times. Its presence can still be felt today in some places.

Ama Lur and *Mari*

The centre of the Basque's traditional cosmic vision has been Earth, which they called Ama Lur (Mother Earth). The extensive underground world teems with life and treasures, a world inhabited by many mythological beings. The Earth's children are the Sun (*Eguzki, ekhi*) and Moon (*ilargi, iretargi, ilazki*, the light of the dead), who return each day to their mother's womb after their daily journey through the skies. Like the Basque language, this world view seems to predate that of the Indo-Europeans, who placed their principal deities in the heavens. For the ancient Basques, the sky was no more than a space of transit, with no special significance in itself.

The main deity of the old pre-Indo-European pantheon is *Mari* , a female spirit that is always associated with an important mountain (e.g. Anboto, Oiz, Gorbeia, Beriain, Putterri, Mondarrain, Orhi, Murumendi and Aloña). Mari is known by many other local names: *Anbotoko Damia, Mariurrika, Putterriko Damea, Orobeko Damea* and *Alonako Gaiztoa*, to cite a few. In the opinion of anthropologist Jose Miguel de Barandiaran, *Mari* is higher than any other Basque spirit. Her powers make her the Earth goddess (*Ama Lur*). She also governs meteorological phenomena, which has led to anthropologist Anuntxi Arana to sustain that she is the goddess of the heavens. Whatever she may be, *Mari* is associated with many caves and the underground world, where she lives. At the same time, she is associated with the climate and the air, because she can fly and is sometimes presented as a flare in the sky. Her mission is to provide justice and punish falsehoods, pride and deceit. In any case, *Mari* is an ambivalent being, a common occurrence in Basque mythology, far from the Manichean

Forest in the mist, in Urkiola (Bizkaia). Below, representation of the sun and stars in a farmhouse.

archetypes introduced by Christianity. Curiously, *Mari* is connected to historical characters: according to some legends, the first lord of Biscay was a child of hers.

The court of *Mari*

The ancient Basque tales populate their world with many other mythological beings, some of which are their own and others shared with other cultures. *Mari*'s husband is *Maju* or *Sugaar* (Snake), who is also considered the father of the first lord of Biscay, and their children are *Atarrabi* and *Mikelats*. To protect the underground world and its treasures, *Mari* and *Maju* often count on the collaboration of the spirits *Zezengorri* (Red Bull) and *Ahari* (Ram).

The country's main forests are inhabited by *Basajaun* (Lord of the forest), who in some areas appears with his female partner, *Basandere*. *Basajaun* is a huge, furry creature that is generally friendly to humans. He is thought to teach farming skills and protect the shepherd's flocks. There are many other spirits as well: *Gaueko*, who comes out at night; the *iratxoak* (the familiar elves); *Aideko* (a haze); the *sorginak* (*Mari*'s assistants, not to be confused with the witches of the same name); and *Ttartalo*, a giant Basque Cyclops who is rather bad tempered. The existence of a serpent-dragon named *Herensuge* or with similar variants, has also been documented in several regions.

The *lamiak* (lamias), beautiful female beings with the duck feet, goat feet or a fish's tail, were also widespread in most of the country. Lamias love water and like to comb their hair on the

Infernuko Erreka (Hell's Trench) runs through Sorginen Lezea (Witches Cave) in Zugarramurdi, the alleged scene of pre-Christian rituals.

Above, a house under the protection of *eguzkilore* and the Sacred Heart. In the centre, a woman in 16th century dress, when women were the principle victims of witch hunts. Below, a *lamia* in the centre of the shield of a farmhouse in Oieregi (Navarre).

shores of streams and pools in the rivers. They say that prayers and the bells in shrines drove them away from some regions.

The *lamiak* are part of the builder spirits, because they were said to have built many bridges, churches and palaces, often in a single night. The *mairuak* were also builders, and so were the *jentilak*, pagan giants of colossal strength who lived on the summits of some mountains. They were in the habit of throwing large boulders. They are said to have erected many megaliths (dolmens and cromlechs). The aura of mystery surrounds the *jentilak*, who are considered to be pre-Christian Basques and others point out that they could be the Indo-Europeans who traversed the country in prehistoric times.

Xorroxin waterfall (Baztan), a place associated with the presence of lamias. Below, large stones with healing properties guard the altar in the church of San Miguel de Arretxinaga (Xemein, Bizkaia).

Celtic, Roman and Christian influences

In addition to the logical evolution of the times, the pre-Indo-European Basque religion was altered by influences from other cultures. This is the case for the emergence of *Urtzi*, a god of the sky that seems to be of Celtic origin. He has left his mark in the Basque names for two days of the week: Thursday (*ortzeguna*, day of *Ortzi*) and Friday (*ortzirala*). According to one chronicle, the Christian God, now called *Jaungoikoa* edo *Jainkoa*, was still named *Urtzia* in the Middle Ages, at least in some areas of the country.

The beautiful cross of Krutziaga (Durango) depicts the sun and moon, as well as Christian elements.

The Romans also seem to have enriched the religious panorama of the Basques. Roman shrines can be found in several places. The Ama Xantalen shrine, in Irun, is built on top of a Roman cemetery. Precisely when Christianity came to Euskal Herria is unknown. José Miguel de Barandiarán claimed that it came late, because the pagan beliefs , in large measure, maintained their force up to the modern age. In any case, Christianity became the predominant and only religion and only, to the extent that the Basque people have had a reputation for being devout Catholics. *Basque fededun* (the Basque is a believer) the saying goes.

The hegemony of Christianity resulted in the disappearance of a part of the earlier pagan beliefs and notable changes in those that remained. Christianity transformed or demonized old local devotions at its convenience, as it did elsewhere. Thus, the Virgin of Arantzazu is perhaps a Christianised version of the *Mari*; the same Mari that is completely demonized in parts of Sakana (Nafarroa), to the point of receiving the name of *Luzifer*. The old beliefs also brought about changes in Basque Christianity. They were so entrenched that some Virgins acquired the characteristics of the *lamiak*, including their ambivalence, as Anuntxi Arana has pointed out.

The sixteenth century witnessed episodes of witch-hunting in several regions of Euskal Herria. The most famous ones took place in the seventeenth century (1609-10), in Lapurdi and in Urdazubi and Zugarramurdi, Nafarroa. One of the underlying reasons seems to be the continuity of pre-Christian rites and beliefs.

BASQUE SPORT, a passion for challenge

Almost all peoples have developed their own sports, tailored to their tastes, their environments and possibilities. In Euskal Herria there are games that seem to be designed specifically for the Basque public; others that may have originated elsewhere but became especially relevant in this country; and a few that are not played anywhere else. Much of the Basque games are everyday work that were transformed into sports when the locals challenged each other. One of the traditional passions of the country have been bets. Any

A pelotari uses the basket in a fronton court.

Two youths play pelota with their bare hands on the fronton courts that pay tribute to Jorge Oteiza in Azkoitia (Gipuzkoa).

job or task could give rise to a challenge that involved people, animals and even nature. The challenges evolved into modalities which ended up taking the form of a sport.

Pelota, the Basque sport par excellence

Almost every civilization in the world has played some sort of ball game. However, there is one game known worldwide as Basque pelota. It may not have been played by Basques only, or even among us, but it is undoubtedly a Basque game. The outline of a *frontón* wall can be seen in every town in the country, however small it may be.

Basque pelota may have evolved from the games played by shepherds in the mountain meadows, thousands of years ago. The place name *pilotaleku* (meaning a place to play ball) is frequent in grazing areas such as Aralar. Although originally played on grass, Basque pelota gradually evolved until it was played on stone. First there were the walls of the churches that served as a front against which a ball could be hit and bounce back. These are the *frontones* known as *plaza-libre*, which are common in Ipar Euskal Herria. Later, the left wall that makes up the current *frontón* court was added. This is the usual model in the four peninsular provinces. There is still another type, the *trinquete*, which has a front wall, a right wall, a *rebote* or back wall, and the left wall with a small overhang. There are many other *pilotalekuak*. Some versions, such as the *laxoa* (glove) require an elongated space with no walls at all.

The *laxoa*, which are now confined to the Baztan-Bidasoa region, are considered the most ancient form of Basque pelota. The players face each other in a manner similar to tennis. It is believed that it was played in mountain grasslands. In the *frontones* with walls and the *trinquetes*, the players use edged baskets (a basket for the *remonte* and a *cesta punta*); several types of bats and even raquets in *xare* and frontenis; or their hands. The later, hand-pelota, is the most important modality. Played barehanded, against a single opponent or between teams of two players, it is practiced by many players in every category and a large number of professional *pelotaris* (pelota players). They compete in three major annual championships: the one for doubles, one for singles inside a "four and a half", and individual against a full *frontón* wall. The latter is the more prestigious and crowns the best *pelotari* at the time. Massif crowds attend these and other tournaments at the site of the *frontón* courts or follow the games on television. Many bets are placed, as well.

There are also professional sportsmen in the basket, bat and *remonte* modalities. In fact, at

the end of the nineteenth century Basque pelota was being played on *frontón* courts in America (Cuba, Venezuela, United States) and even Asia (China, the Philippines and Indonesia), always associated with bets. Basque pelota is in decline, however, and has lost the brilliance of the games played in the magic triangle made up by Gernika, Markina and Durango.

It was the king of sports among the Basques until the arrival of football. Travelers like Humboldt echoed its social importance in an era in which the great *bertsolaris* published rhymed chronicles of memorable games. Verses by *Udarregi*, *Txirrita*, *Oxalde* and many others from the eighteenth century onwards, who glorified such heroes of the frontón as Jose Inda *Perkain*, from Aldude; *Mankua*, from Villabona; and Benito *Sugarri*, from Markina. The list extends up to the living legends, including one who deserves a place of honour; Julian Retegi.

Rowing, a challenge with the men and nature

As irrefutable evidence of the concerns and interests of the Basques, the *bertso paperak* (sheets of verses) praise other sports, apart from the pelota games. Chief among them are the rowing regattas (*traineru estropadak*). The only record of the oldest regattas are the verses that were composed to the greater glory of the winners on occasion of a competition between rowers in Ondarroa and Lekeitio (1854).

The traineras were originally wooden boats propelled by oars and sometimes sailing, used for fishing a range of species, from the anchovies to whales. In those tasks was vital to be the first to arrive at a bank of fish or to collect a captured whale. It was equally important to return to port as quickly as possible to fetch a good price for the catches. In this type of activity was inevitable that the crews should challenge each other.

The challenges attracted large crowds in the second half of the nineteenth century, when they began to evolve as a sport, a modality of rowing with a fixed bench. The first races were held, the most important of which is the Bandera de La Concha, in Donostia, held for the first time in 1879. It is still the most prestigious regatta and attracts the most crowds. It is held on the first Sunday of September.

Currently the traineras are made of *kevlar* and carbon fibre. The crews are composed of thirteen oarsmen and a cox who guides the boat

Three vessels in action in the main trainera regatta, the flag of La Concha.

from the stern. The regattas cover a distance of three nautical miles (5,556 meters) which include one or three turns (*ziaboga*) around a buoy. Two smaller boats are also used in competitions: the *trainerillas* (six rowers and cox) and the *bateles* (four rowers and cox).

Apart from the Bandera de la Concha, many other regattas are held in summer in the coastal communities (some in the estuaries and others in the open sea). Some are included in the ACT League (Association of Trainera Clubs), the first division of rowing, in which a growing number of Basque, Galician and Cantabrian participate. Women rowers have recently created their own league under the ACT (since 2009) and hold their own Bandera de la Concha (since 2008).

The winning team, in this case Kaiku from Sestao, holding the flag but still on the water, celebrating their victory.

Herri kirolak, a homage to ancient tasks

If on the coast the *arrantzaleak* (fishermen) rowed hard to bring home a wage, the farmers in the villages were not idle. Incredibly demanding physical work gave rise to the emergence of challenges that gradually turned into sports known as herri kirolak, or country sports. Although they have not been highly developed, the challenges still play an important role, and are included in championships, exhibitions and competitions. The challenges arise when an athlete launches a challenge and backs it up with a certain amount of money, which anyone who accepts the challenge must match.

The challenges still take place among the *aizkolariak*, the log splitters. The heirs of loggers and charcoal burners who were in charge of cutting down trees to feed the shipyards and ironworks, the *aizkolaris* will stand on a thick log (usually beech) and, without pause, chop at it with an axe until it splits into two halves. The task usually lasts half an hour, during which they cut several logs, although in some challenges they may employ up to two hours. This sport is also practiced in countries like the United States, Canada, Australia or New Zealand, although under different conditions. In Euskal Herria there is a championship that has several categories (depending on the quality of the participants), in addition to a league, *Urrezko Aizkora* (Golden Axe), which has held competitions since 1999.

Stone lifting is another popular sport, practiced by the *harrijasotzaileak*. This is a test of strength in which the athlete lifts a stone of great

Above, a woman participating in a txinga erute (weight lifting) contest. On the right, an aizkolari's axe cuts into a tree trunk.

A harrijasotzaile lives a cubic stone weighing 200 kilos.

weight that can have cylindrical, cubic, spherical or rectangular shape. The stone must be lifted until it is level with the shoulder to score. The stone lifter who manages to lift more stones within a given time limit wins the contest. Of course, the stones they call small (100-125 kilos) are the ones that can be lifted faster and more often. Only four *harrijasotzailesak*, Iñaki Otegi *Gibitegi*, Iñaki Perurena, Inaxio Perurena and Mikel Saralegi have lifted stones weighing

300 kilos. The current record is held by Saralegi, who lifted a stone weighing 329 kilos. Iñaki Perurena boasts another extraordinary record: in 1999, he made one thousand lifts with a stone weighing 100 kilos in 5 hours and four minutes.

Other modalities of *herri kirolak* are not exclusive of Euskal Herria, as in the case of the *sega-proba* (cutting grass in a meadow with a scythe); *soka-tira*, tug-of-war; and some have been lost, such as the Basque "javelin" throw, in which a bar was thrown instead of a javelin. Other sports have been recovered, like the *harri-zulatzailea* championships, in which shot-firers drilled blast holes in the mines of Biscay to place sticks of dynamite.

Contests with animals

The farming tasks at the origin of Basque sports meant that animals were often involved in the competitions as well. Dogs, oxen, horses, donkeys, sheep and rams were commonly used in traditional sports. Some of them were used in dragging games. The aim was to move a large stone from one spot to another in a special square called a *probaleku* (testing ground). The team that managed to drag a stone weighing 1,500-5,000 kilos the furthest within a given time won. Oxen were normally used for the dragging competitions (*idi probak*), although sometimes horses (*zaldi probak*), donkeys (*asto probak*) and even people (*gizon probak*) did the dragging. In general, farm festivals and agricultural fairs still remain a source of many bets and also a certain degree of controversy, as a consequence of the fact that the sensitivity on the rights of animals has increased in recent decades.

The sheepdog championships arrived in Euskal Herria in 1955, when the first trial of that sort was held in Oñati. The idea was imported but it was well suited to the Basque's deep-rooted herding tradition. Since then it has spread throughout the country, and today provincial championships, national and even international are held. The shepherds must Every pastor should ensure that your dog enter the sheep in the sheepfold in the shortest possible time and without penalty.

The Basque footprint in sports

Above, view of the new Athletic Club soccer stadium (San Mames), on the day of a game. Below, Biaritz Olympique fans celebrate a title (2005) with the players.

Given that Euskal Herria has no state of its own, and both France and Spain ban Basque teams from entering official sports competitions, Basque presence in international sports is often labelled as Spanish or French. However, the movement in favour of the Basque teams is strong, and in some minority sports they have been able to normalize their participation. They are still working on a legal level to get support for a widespread bid to be allowed to participate.

The three most popular sports in the country are football, rugby and cycling. The football was introduced in the nineteenth century, especially by the upper classes from Bilbao who studied in England. The sport spread rapidly to every

Left, a cyclist from the Euskaltel-Euskadi team in the Tour de France.
Above, followers of the Osasuna.
Below, museum of the Real Sociedad.

social class. By the 1920s, football was already as popular as Basque pelota, which until then was second to none. The Basque to football has been the care taken to select a source of young players, of which the Basque clubs are a good example (Athletic, Real Sociedad, Osasuna and so forth). The Athletic is one of the few clubs in the world that only signs local players to their team since 1910. The team boasts eight League championships and 23 Cup trophies. It has been runner-up of the UEFA Cup twice and has produced such myths as Rafael Moreno *Pitxitxi*, Telmo Zarraonandia *Zarra* and José Angel Iribar, *El Chopo*. The Real Sociedad has wone the League twice and two Cups. Its greatest feat was to reach the semi-finals of the 1982-83 European Cup. Since 1987, when the Real Sociedad won the Cup, no Basque team has achieved an official title in the men's category. The same is not true for women's football, which in recent years has emerged with force in the Basque scene. The Athletic has won the Super League four times (in 2002-2007) and in some games it has attracted more than 25,000 spectators.

In Ipar Euskal Herria the favourite sport is rugby. Two clubs share the glory. One is the Aviron Bayonnais, who won its first French championship in 1913 and has maintained its prestige for more than a century in spite of a fall from the First Division (currently it is in the Top 14) in 1996-2004. The other is the Biarritz Olympique, which won several titles in the 1930s and experienced a golden age in the early twenty-first century by winning three French championships in 2002-2005) and one European championship in 2012. Despite the fact that Ipar Euskal Herria has a population of only 280,000 out of a total population of 65 million in France, there have always been Basque players on the powerful French team, from legendary Andre Behoteguy to most recent idol, Imanol Harinordoki.

Lastly, no review of Basque sport would be complete without mentioning cycling. The Basque Country has given more to the sport than great athletes like Miguel Indurain and Jesus Loroño, and memorable races on Basque roads that showcased stars like Eddy Merckx. The sport has also attracted thousands of followers who throng to line the roads and cheer the cyclists as they race by. The vivid performances in the Pyrenean stages of the Tour in recent years are merely the most extreme expressions of what can be experienced in any race in the Basque mountains. For twenty years the Euskadi team, whose members are all Basque, kept the passion for cycling alive, in a romantic dream that took shape as a reality. The project ended in 2013, but the fondness for this epic sport does not diminish.

BASQUE ART, modest beauty

Pio Baroja said that "the Basque Country has no great historical monuments, nor majestic architecture, nor memories of past events that may be more or less sensational with which to receive the travellers who choose to visit it. Its heritage is modest, yet subtle". He was right. There are no spectacular Gothic cathedrals that impress the visitor, or colossal castles, nor Sistine Chapels that are a worldwide point of reference. Ours has been a country poor in general, without a state of its own, with no big cities or immense fortunes. Here everything is measured. Art also. But there is no lack of art. From Prehistoric times to the twenty-first century, the country has accumulated a modest heritage. Modest but subtle, "to gain the admiration of sensitive people", insisted Baroja.

Rock paintings in the Santimamiñe cave (Kortezubi, Bizkaia).

Early hidden art

The oldest artistic monuments in the country are hidden in the remote darkness of a dozen caves. They are paintings and engravings which, in some cases, date back to the early days of the Upper Paleolithic period, more than 35,000 years ago, although the majority belong to the Magdalenian period (11,000 years ago). The horses in Ekain, the bison in Santimamiñe, carved pieces in Izturitze (including its famous *txistu*) and the pendants in Praileaitz are part of the current cultural imagination of the Basques.

The same could be said of the megalithic monuments that dot much of the country, especially in the mountain areas. Cromlechs, dolmens and menhirs are essential elements of the landscape: the Sorginetxe Dolmens, La Chabola de la Hechicera (The Hut of the Sorceress)(both in Araba); Mairietxe (Nafarroa Beherea), Arrako and Farangortea (Nafarroa); cromlechs like the ones in Okabe (Nafarroa Beherea), Auza

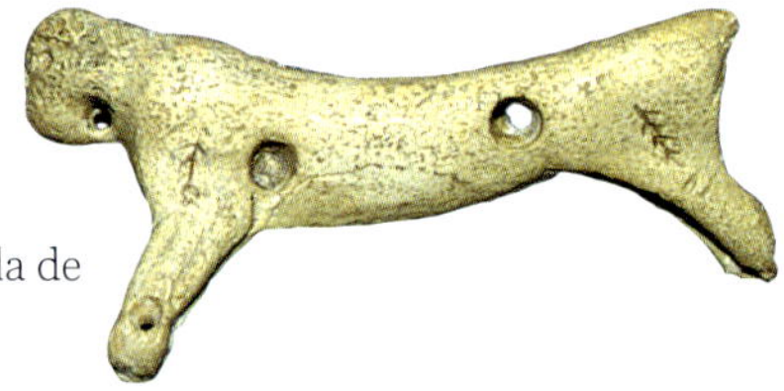

An animal figure carved in bone, found in the Izturitze cave (Nafarroa Beherea).

(Nafarroa) and Mugarriluze (Legaire, Araba); and menhirs in Kurutzegane (Gorbeia, Bizkaia), more than five meters tall. Very close to the hut of La Chabola de la Hechicera, in La Hoya (Laguardia), an Iron Age settlement with paved streets, houses in adobe and stone, and even a large cistern represents the most perfect example of a Neolithic fortified settlement.

With the Romans, art was transferred from caves and mountains to the urban centres and rural towns. The first cities emerged: Iruña-Veleia (Araba), Oiasso (Irun, Gipuzkoa), Lapurdum (Bayonne), Forua (Bizkaia), Andelos (Mendigorria, Nafarroa) and the newly localized Iturissa (Auritz, Nafarroa); and rural properties like the town of Liédena. The Romans also built the huge circular tower that crowns the solitary summit of the Urkulu mountain (1,419 m), in the Pyrenees of Navarre.

The Middle Ages, discrete splendour

The land became rural again after the fall of the Roman Empire. That is why the following traces of the Basque Country's modest art is to be found in isolated places, like the series of artificial caves in Trebiñu and Valdegobia, and the necropolis of Argiñeta (Elorrio).

The most important examples of Basque medieval art, however, are closely linked to the

Circular tower that stands on the summit of mount Urkulu (Orbaizeta, Navarre, 1,419 m). It appears to be a Roman monument.

Kingdom of Navarre and the Camino de Santiago (St Jame's Way). French and Romanesque influences followed the Way into the Basque Country, bringing unique works of art, like the lovely church of Santa Grazi and the exotic parish of Ospitalepea (Zuberoa), declared a World Heritage Site; the crypt and *Speciosa* door in the monastery in Leire; the spectacular porch of the church Santa María la Real, in Zaragoza, and the odd shrine in Eunate (all three are in Nafarroa); and the basilica of San Prudencio de Armentia, in Gasteiz.

Gothic art appeared first in Nafarroa and Ipar Euskal Herria, with works of admirable beauty like the cathedrals of Tutera (transition from Romanesque to Gothic), Baiona (magnificent; a designated World Heritage site), Iruñea and Gasteiz. The Gothic style came later in Bizkaia and Gipuzkoa, as the towns grew larger and churches were built, like the ones in Balmaseda, Lekeitio, Deba and Hondarribia. The Gothic style also left its imprint on civil architecture, consisting mostly of noble palaces and tower houses, built for defensive purposes as well has habitation: the Luzea Tower in Zarautz, the tower of Kexaa in Aiara, the medieval old town of Vitoria, the Muñatones tower (Muskiz) and the Donamaria

Spectacular indoor view of the cathedral of Santa María, in Gasteiz.

The church of Ospitalepea (Zuberoa), declared an UNESCO World Heritage site, is a blend of the Roman and Byzantine styles (12th century). Below, statues from the church in Guardia (Araba).

and Olkotz towers, in Nafarroa. The castle-palace of Erriberri-Olite is especially worthy of mention.

In the sixteenth century, more silver was needed to finance sumptuous churches built in the Plateresque style, at first, and later in the Basque Gothic style, a local version of the predominant Renaissance current of that period. Magnificent churches were erected in that era, like the churches in Bergara, Elorrio and Begoña, and the monastery of Iratxe, in addition to a large part of the defensive bastions in Iruñea, the beautiful University of Oñati and the unique Trinitarian churches (crowned by steeples with three vertices) in Zuberoa.

The first known Basque painters and sculptors were from that period, like Juan de Antxieta, the author of numerous altarpieces, and Francisco Mendieta, the painter from Alava.

Detail of the Roman façade of Santa María la Real, in Zangoza (NAFARROA)

The Romanesque chapel of San Vicentejo (Trebiñu, ARABA).

Wood sculptures in the church of La Antigua, in Zumarraga (GIPUZKOA)

Spectacular Romanesque façade of the cathedral of Tutera (NAFARROA)

Romanesque chapel of Eunate (Muruzabal, NAFARROA) boasts a surprising octagonal layout.

The Gothic cathedral of Baiona (LAPURDI), seen from the cloister.

Beautiful star on the ceiling of the Gothic church of San Severino (Balmaseda, BIZKAIA).

art Middle Ages

The Baroque period

The Baroque style had a more profound influence in the country, despite the fact that it appeared in the seventeenth century, when the economy was hardly conducive to works of art. The Counter-Reformation brought the curved lines and the profuse baroque decorations and the religious orders followed the new aesthetic canon when they built their convents. The most important work of art was the basilica of Loiola, a superb building built around the house tower of the family of San Ignacio, which has been preserved in its interior. The towers, chapels and altarpieces of many Basque churches are in the Baroque style, although the main part of the building may be built in other styles.

Inside the Casa de Juntas (Meeting House) in Gernika. Below, Constitution square (Donostia).

Above, the Donostia Yacht Club, in the Rationalist style. On the right, the sanctuary of Loiola.

As far as civil architecture is concerned, the nobility filled the country with proud palaces that replaced the old, uncomfortable house towers. Some of the palaces are still standing in Elorrio, Markina and Zurbao, in Araba, and in Iruñea's old town. Many town councils were also built during the Baroque period.

The late eighteenth century and early nineteenth century witnessed a return to the classical forms (Neoclassicism) and a preference for straight lines. This period left some highly monumental architecture, like the palace of Navarre and the façade of the cathedral of Santa Maria (both in Iruñea); the aqueduct in Noain; the new squares in Gasteiz, Donostia and Bilbao, and the church of Santa Maria in Bermeo.

From a medieval past to the vanguards

In the following years, the Romantic atmosphere brought about a new interpretation of the mediaeval forms that is easily recognisable in the towers and palaces that were built or re-built in the nineteenth century, like the ones in Butroe and Arteaga (Bizkaia) and Abbadia (Hendaia). The same could be said of the new cathedral in Gasteiz. Despite the Neo-Medieval taste, the widening of the capitals was designed according to the most stringent bourgeois criteria with regards to the occupation of space. In the early twentieth century, eclecticism appeared to predominate, but soon after came the influence of the European avant-garde. It showed in the

Sculpture of Oteiza playing with spherical shapes and a vacuum (Bilbao).

architecture, with modernism (the transporter bridge in Bizkaia), art déco (the Casino in Biarritz) and rationalism (the Yacht Club in Donostia). A new style also developed, the Neo-Basque, in an attempt to combine the new architecture with certain traits taken from the farmhouses. It can be seen in the palace of Ibaigane (Bilbao) and the house of Edmond Rostand, Villa Arnaga, in Kanbo (Lapurdi).

Basque fine arts are best represented by the paintings that flourished in the late nineteenth century. Dario Regoyos and Adolfo Guiard broke with the prevailing academic art and went out in the search for light with sensitivity of the impressionists. Their landscapes created the most typical image of Euskal Herria: the romantic rural life and the industrious urban life.

The path they opened was followed by many great painters, each with their own style and subject matter, but all open to the plethora of avant-garde movements at the time. Ignacio Zuloaga, Aurelio Arteta, the Arrue brothers, Jean Paul Tillac, Ciga, Francisco Iturrino, Gustavo de Maeztu, Antonio Gezala and Nicolas Lecuona belong to a long list of authors who created the country's pictorial imagination and left a remarkable legacy in galleries such as the Museum of Fine Arts in Bilbao.

The civil war put an end to the golden age of Basque painting and the subsequent dictatorship abandoned the fine arts to rot. In that difficult time sculptors took over, especially the great Jorge Oteiza, who attained international recognition in the São Paulo Biennial (1957) and overcame his initial expressionism to venture into the abstract. Oteiza was decisive for his theories on Basque art (especially in his book *Quousque tandem*) that motivated a new generation of artists and intellectuals concerned with recovering Basque culture, until then reviled and even persecuted.

The Museum of Fine Arts, in Bilbao, holds an splendid artistic legacy inside and outside of the building.

A Basque festival, dancing in the Antiguo, San Sebastián, the work of Darío Regoyos.

The other great sculptor of the time was Eduardo Chilida, awarded in various international competitions and the author of interventions that combine art and public space. Perhaps his most famous work is *Haizearen Orrazia* (the Wind Comb), in the west end of the San Sebastian bay of La Concha. Oteiza and Chillida each have a museum; the Oteiza museum in Altzuza, Nafarroa, and the Chillida Leku, in Hernani.

A classical sculpture on a street in Donostia.

The two sculptors collaborated on the most referential Basque architectural work of the twentieth century, the new basilica of Arantzazu (Oñati, 1950-54). The architectural design was the work of Francisco Javier Sáenz de Oiza, from Navarre. The intervention of Oteiza is substantiated in the doorway, with a piety and fourteen apostles that, prohibited by the Church, were not placed until 1969. The renowned artists Nestor Basterretxea and Xabier Álvarez de Eulate also collaborated. The altarpiece is the work of Lucio Muñoz, from Madrid.

The new school of Basque artists has left an extensive legacy of authors and works, both in the field of painting (Rafael Ruiz Balerdi, José Luis Zumeta, Jesus Mari Lazkano, Xabier Morras) and sculpture (Remigio Mendiburu, Koldobika Jauregi, Ricardo Ugarte and Dora Salazar). Agustín Ibarrola has developed both genres, but his most famous work is his pictorial intervention in a pine forest in Kortezubi (the Oma forest).

Basque architecture in recent years has been marked by emblematic creations in the heart of the main cities. The most well known example is the Guggenheim Museum in Bilbao, the work of Frank Gehry. Its dizzying curved forms and skin of titanium made it a global phenomenon before it was even completed. Basque architecture has come a long way since the modest beauty described at the beginning of this chapter. The new times are represented by conference halls such as the Kursaal (Donostia), Baluarte (Iruñea) and Euskalduna (Bilbao); and the Iberdrola tower (Bilbao, 165 meters).

Sculptures in the Artium museum (Gasteiz).

Portugalete and the transporter bridge (Bizkaia).

Guggenheim Museum Bilbao

art

contemporary art

Abandoibarra, Bilbao.

Sculptures of the Apostles in the chapel of Arantzazu (Gipuzkoa), the work of Oteiza.

A room in the Museum of Fine Arts, in Bilbao

Forest of Oma (Bizkaia), the pictorial work of Agustín Ibarrola.

Villa Arnaga (Kanbo), Lapurdi.

Basque SHOWS

In Euskal Herria, people like music, all kinds of music and love to share it with friends. That is why there is no town, no matter how small, without some sort of musical ensemble: choirs, choral societies, choirs of eight voices, municipal bands and rock groups. Until recently, the local customers (*txikiteros*) were in the habit of singing Basque songs in the bars, as well.

To the Basque beat

Music and song have always played a major role in Euskal Herria. As the lyrics of the *jota* say, "A people who sing does not die". The jota is a genre of music associated with dance. Another jota says that two men made Navarra immortal, "the renowned Sarasate, and Gayarre, the man from Roncal". In the nineteenth century a group of musicians from Navarre set a high standard: composers Hilarión Eslava and Emilio Arrieta, the violinist Pablo Sarasate and, perhaps above all, the tenor Julian Gayarre, the shepherd from Roncal who astonished audiences in the Scala of Milan and other opera houses with his voice. The other beacon from that period shone very briefly: Juan Crisóstomo Arriaga, known as the Basque Mozart, died in 1826 at the age of 20,

after having composed the opera *Los Esclavos Felices* (The Happy Slaves).

In the first quarter of the twentieth century, the most international of the Basque composers was Maurice Ravel, from Ziburu (Lapurdi), the creator of the famous Bolero. Another outstanding composer is Alava Jesus Guridi, author of the opera *Amaya* and *Diez Melodías Vascas* (Ten Basque Melodies), based on Basque folk music. Other popular musicians were José María Usandizaga, known for his opera *Mendi-Mendiyan*, and Aita Donostia, who composed the opera *Larraldeko Lorea* and was a collector of Basque folklore. The latest opera is *Gernika* (1986), by the master from Zarautz, Francisco Escudero. The twentieth century produced other important composers, such as Pablo Sorozábal, Carmelo Bernaola, Anton Larrauri and Luis de Pablo, while other musicians have gained well-deserved international recognition: at the piano, Jesus Atxukarro and the sisters Katia and Marielle Labeque; harpist Nicanor Zabaleta and the sopranos Ainhoa Arteta and Maria Bayo, as well as various choirs, including the Orfeón Donostiarra, a choral society.

Currently, Euskal Herria boasts three symphony orchestras, one each in Euskadi and Bilbao, and the Pablo Sarasate orchestra, in Navarre. There is also an opera season run by the Bilbao Friends of the Opera Society (ABAO), and prestigious festivals such as the Musical Fortnight in Donostia.

Apart from classical music, many excellent music festivals are planned throughout the year. The jazz festivals held in Donostia, Gasteiz, Baiona and Getxo offer a broad range of music.

On the preceding page, Basque instruments (bagpipes, txanbela, alboka and several types of accordions). Above, street performance by the txistularis from Donostia.

Basque folk music played with local instruments has always been highly important as well, with the melodies often associated with classical music. In most parts of the country dances and acts in the public square have been accompanied by the *txistu*, the Basque version of the flute of three holes (there is another variant, more high-pitched, called the *txirula*). Is often accompanied by the *silbote* (a larger flute) and the *atabal*, a drum that provides the rhythm. The *txistu* players (*txistulariak*) use their left hand for the flute while playing another small percussion instrument with the right, which is usually a small drum, although the *ttun-ttun* (psaltery) is still played in the Pyrenees area. Currently, the txistu is played in parades, pilgrimages and dance exhibitions.

The second most common indigenous instrument in the public square is the dulzaina, a local instrument of the oboe family. Historically, it was played in all of the country and the rest of the Mediterranean basin. Soule/Zuberoa developed its own version, the *txanbela*, which has been on the verge of disappearing. After years of disuse, the dulzaina now accompanies the masquerade of giants, is played in the street

Above, two young people pay a txalaparta on the pavement. Below, Mikel Laboa

dances (*pasacalles*) and puts the music to some traditional dances, such as Otsagabia.

There was a time when the *romerías* (religious processions followed by festivities) were held to the music of the *alboka*, a shepherd's instrument that was very difficult to master. Formed by two bull horns joined by a body of wood, it is of Arabic origin, although it became very popular in several parts of Europe in the Middle Ages. In Euskal Herria it was preserved in Bizkaia, from where it has been recovered.

Another instrument that was recovered when it was about to fall into oblivion is the *txalaparta*, a percussion instrument consisting of several boards that are beaten rhythmically with four sticks. It was preserved in the region of the rivers Urumea and Oria, linked to the production of cider. Today it is so pervasive that it has been played in everything from political events to Madonna's tour.

Few instruments express the joyful spirit of the people in the Basque Country than the *trikitixa*, a small diatonic accordion that was imported from Italy in the mid-nineteenth century and soon became popular. It was condemned by the Church, some of whose ministers called it *infernuko auspoa* (the bellows from hell). The *trikitixa*, like the *alboka*, is often accompanied by a tambourine, although at present the variety is vast. In the mid-80s, Joseba Tapia and Kepa Junkera promoted the instrument and, with their innovative contribution, transmitted it to the new generations. This small accordion has proved to be highly versatile and today is used by groups that play all sorts of music.

There is no curse

The 1960s heralded a new form of popular music, incarnated in the singer-songwriters that gave rise to Euskal Kantagintza Berria (the new Basque song). The most noted singers of this movement joined the cultural group *Ez dok amairu* ("there is no thirteen"), an expression that should be construed as having broken a curse. They combined the popular tradition with new poetry created by ground-breaking musicians like Joxan Artze and Jose Angel Irigarai, as well as new aesthetics propounded by artists like Jorge Oteiza and José Luis Zumeta.

The longest and most successful careers were those of Mikel Laboa, sublime when interpreting popular themes; the master of experimentation, Benito Lertxundi, a bard of the twentieth century (and also of the twenty-first); and Xabier Lete, who boasts a powerful lyrical streak. That

Hertzainak, Benito Lertxundi,
Lourdes Iriondo and Kortatu

rebellious movement took root in a broad segment of the public and was wildly popular.

This new beginning of contemporary musicians continued in the 70s with singers Imanol, Gorka Knörr and Txomin Artola, among many others.

In parallel, a new folk current was developing in Bilbao with groups such as Oskorri, intimately related to the transgressive social poet Gabriel Aresti.

At the same time, the rich voices Pantxo eta Peio, Erramun Martikorena, Jean Mixel Bedasagar and Anje Duhalde were being heard in Iparralde.

Euskal Herria rock

The new rhythms that marked the beat of popular music worldwide arrived in the 1970s. Rock n' roll was heard in Basque for the first time in the voice of Niko Etxart and soon produced high quality music, like the album *Ametsaren Bidea*, by Errobi. Composer and singer Ruper Ordorika burst on the scene in the late 70s with a pop-rock song linked to a new poetic movement led by the writer Bernardo Atxaga. In the 80s, an period of effervescence, saw new bars open where music was played; the music industry became more professional; new bands and styles appeared and, best of all, a great many concerts that attracted huge audiences. It was the era of Radical Basque Rock, a label not always accepted by the bands themselves, which included the rock of Barricada, the pure punk of RIP, the essential punk of La Polla Records and the ska-punk-rock of Kortatu, in Spanish; and the punk-rock of Zarama and the electrifying rhythms of Hertzainak in Basque. From then on, rock was on the road with punk, heavy, ska...

The Kukai troupe create contemporary choreographies based on traditional dance.

and the Basque language was present in all of it. Another trend in the late 70s opted for pop. Its greatest exponent was Itoiz, a band group that defined the musical tendencies of several generations of Basques with their themes, sometimes intimate and thoughtful, sometimes festive and catchy.

The 90s began with the unprecedented Negu Gorriak, a band that innovated hip-hop in Basque and gave way to an active movement of groups close to the new crossover trends, in which hardcore, rap and funk were mixed with a band's own roots, launching protest songs with an anti-establishment attitude.

Today there are bands like Ken Zazpi, Gatibu, Esne Beltza, Zea Mays, Su ta Gar or Berri Txarrak and singers as Gari, Anari, Fermin Muguruza, Mikel Urdangarin, Rafa Rueda or Petti who thrill their audience in Basque.

Ken Zazpi's pop rock has made the band highly popular in recent years.

The whole movement of popular music that began in the 60's created genuine classics that are still played on radio stations and in festivals. Modern groups make versions of them and they are even sung at social gatherings. Some of these classics are Mikel Laboa's *Txoria Txori*, Itoiz's *Lau Teilatu*, Benito Lertxundi's *Oi ama Euskal Herria*, Xabier Lete's *Xalbadorren Heriotzean*, Hertzainak's *Aitormena* and Kortatu's *Sarri, Sarri*.

In a country dance

Voltaire referred to the Basques as a people that not only sings but also dances on both sides of the Pyrenees. The Basques and their dances have been appreciated "since always" in the international panorama of dance. The *pas de basque*, incorporated into the classical ballet, bears witness to this.

Just as they did with the *trikitixa*, there was a time when priests and monks persecuted public dances as sinful and incitement to lust. Currently, with no one persecuting them,

A moment in the play Ubera Gorriak, by the Kabia group, in the community house in Intxaurrondo (Donostia).

many cultural groups are working hard to recover popular participation in the dances of festivals and pilgrimages. In the places where they still have a relevant and symbolic role, these dances are in good health: *Kaixarranka* in Lekeitio, *Zubi gaineko dantza* in Lesaka, *Mahai gainekoa* in Xemein, the *maskaradak* in Zuberoa and the dances of Otsagabia... Any act that seeks a degree of solemnity requires an aurresku of honor.

There are multitudinous dances (*biribilketak, porrusaldak, kalejirak*), in which sticks and swords are used (the latter are the classical, spectacular *ezpatadantza*). Women have recently joined the dances performed at important social events, in which they could not participate before (*mutil-dantza* in Baztan). Prominent specialists such as Juan Antonio Urbeltz have made a great effort to adapt Basque dances to present-day society and recover old dances.

In the field of contemporary dance several troupes stand out: the Ballet Biarritz (created in 1988); groups of innovators like Kukai, who combine tradition and modernity under the direction of Jon Maya; and dancers like Lucia Lakarra, Itziar Mendizábal and Igor Yebra, who have gained considerable international recognition.

Performing Arts, an old hobby

Documented theatre in the Basque language goes back almost as far back as Basque literature. The oldest record is from 1494, the year when the monarchs of Navarre, John of Albret and Catherine de Foix, were feted at various celebrations on the occasion of their coronation. The celebrations included at least one play in the Basque language, of which only one song remains. There is a record of religious works in different parts of the country, such as Leintz-Gatzaga (1510) and Ibero (early nineteenth century). Some signature works, such as *Gabonetako Ikuskizuna*, by Peter Ignazio Barrutia (1750) have also been preserved. In dealing with literature, we have mentioned some highlights of Basque theatre in nineteenth and early twentieth centuries. We have also reviewed the long history of the Soule pastorals, representatives of a popular theatre that was deeply rooted in the country. Good proof of this is provided by the broad range of rituals and burlesque performances documented in Euskal Herria: *cencerradas* (noise made with cowbells on festive occasions), *galarrotsak, zintzarrotsak, tobera-mustrak, asto-lasterrak* and *karroxak*. The parodies of trials in those rituals were inserted in the carnivals and other festivities.

That was the popular vein that encouraged authors of the 60s, such as Gabriel Aresti, to work with youth groups and young actors to create ground-breaking works against the Francoist repression and conventional morality. Despite the fact that subsequently other renowned authors like Bernardo Atxaga (*Henry Bengoa Inventarium*, 1986) have occasionally contributed to this area of the Basque literature, the genre has become much less popular.

Contemporary theatre in Basque suffers from the disadvantages resulting from the situation of the language, but it enjoys a certain tradition, is less burdened with strictly commercial productions, and attracts young talent that is willing to experiment with new, bolder approaches. Groups such as Maskarada, Kukubiltxo, Tanttaka and Antzerkiola Imaginarioa have produced and played works that have marked an epoch in the country. In Ipar Euskal Herria, the tradition of amateur theatre remains strong and continues carry productions in the Basque language to every region. Street theatre has experienced a remarkable increase and popular recognition for the quality of its troupes (Deabru Beltzak, for example), and the attractive festivals in Lekeitio and Bilbao.

Love of cinema

Euskal Herria has had close ties with the cinema almost since the invention of the cinematograph. The first screenings can be traced back to 1896 in locations such as Donostia, Biarritz, Iruñea and Bilbao. In Bilbao, the first cinema was opened in 1905. Among the short films being screened on the opening day there was one depicting a training session of the city's football club, the Athletic, in the Lamiako stadium. We owe many early films such as Josetxo (1916), *Edurne, modista bilbaina, El Mayorazgo de Basterretxe* (1927) and *Euzkadi* (1933) to the first film producers. The country also aroused the interest of foreign film-makers, from Nazis like Herber Brieger (*In Lande der Basken*, 1941) to geniuses like Orson Welles (*The Land of the Basques*, 1955).

After the Franco dictatorship, a number of films were produced in the Castilian language under the label of Basque Cinema, which had a significant impact, with titles such as Imanol Uribe's *La Fuga de Segovia*, Pedro Olea's *Akelarre*, and Montxo Armendariz's *Tasio*. These directors, along with younger ones like Julio Medem and Alex de la Iglesia, continue to enjoy recognition. The same is true of a plethora of actors, actresses and film professionals. Some of them are highly renowned in the international scene, like the director of photography Javier Aguirresarobe and composer Alberto Iglesias.

However, the country has not been able to create an industry of its own, largely due to the small size of its market. Therefore, Basque productions depend on foreign industries, especially the Spanish ones.

Film buffs are portrayed in the festivals held in several cities, particularly in the Basque capitals. The most renowned festival of all is the Zinemaldia San Sebastian Film Festival, created in 1953. Held in September, it has become a cultural and social event, not only because it attracts Hollywood stars but also for the huge attendance by the general public. The capital of Gipuzkoa also hosts other festivals (the

On the preceding page, posters of some of the films shot in Basque in recent years. Above these lines, a press conference by Zinemaldia, with John Travolta, Oliver Stone, Benicio del Toro and Edurne Ormazabal.

Fantasy and Horror Film Week, the Film and Human Rights Festival, and so forth). Biarritz organises two important film events, one dedicated to Latin American productions and the other to multimedia. Bilbao's International Documentary and Short Films Festival – Zinebi – grows more important every year, like the International GayLesboTrans Film and Theatre Festival – Zinegoak – and the Fantasy Film Festival. Bilbao also holds an International Festival of Mountain Films – Mendifilm – and an International Invisible Film Festival, as well as the Future Shorts Festival. Iruñea also boasts Short Films Festival. Film productions in the Basque language have had their own festival since 1978: Lekeitioko Bideo eta Zine Bilera.

Moreover, the possibility of seeing feature length films in the Basque language is scarce. In 1968, the documentary *Ama Lur*, by Nestor Basterretxea and Fernando Larruquert, created a huge stir, for many reasons. The early years of the transition brought the film series Ikuska, which was greatly encouraged by Antxon Ezeiza, himself a director of films such as *Ke arteko egunak* (1989). Other films date from the same period, such as *Hamaseigarrenean Aidanez*, *Erreporteroak* and *Kareletik*. There is also *Kalabaza tripontzia*, by Juanba Berasategi, a pioneer of animation, a genre that, always within the limits of the country, has had continuity and gained some recognition.

The Basque language made its big screen début in the first decade of the twenty-first century with fiction films, always few and far between but not without some successes such as *Aupa Etxebeste!* (Asier Altuna and Telmo Esnal, 2005) and *Kutsidazu bidea, Ixabel* (Fernando Bernués and Mireia Gabilondo, 2006), *Izarren argia* (Mikel Rueda, 2010) *Amaren eskuak* (Gabilondo, 2013) and Loreak (Garaño-Goenaga, 2014).

Other areas such as animation cinema, mentioned earlier, documentaries and short films are highly interesting efforts. In 1997 producer Baleuko won the Goya award for best animation feature film with *Megasonicos*.

FESTIVALS and TRADITIONS

It could be said that a people shows the face with which they would like to be known with their festivities. The Basque festive schedule, in addition to fun, reflects a large part of the traditions, values and aspirations that permeate broad sectors of society. The defence of the country's own identity, the Basque language, updated traditions and exciting future projects are reflected in festive events that span the entire calendar.

The most important festivities in winter are related to the carnival (*inauteriak*, *aratusteak*), in both its urban and rural version. Logically, the capitals stand out in the urban festivities, especially in places like Toulouse. The origin of the *tamborrada* in Donostia was a manifestation of the carnival. In the rural festivities, the flamboyance of the *maskaradak* (carnival) in Zuberoa is spectacular. It is held from February to April, in a different location every Sunday. The *zanpantzar* in Zubieta and Ituren, and the carnival in Lantz are also interesting. Each carnival has its atavistic characters

The Kezka troupe during a carnival in a rural area of Eibar.

Running of the bulls in the Sanfermines in Iruñea. The most well-known festival in Euskal Herria combines the risk of running the bulls with an excellent ambience.

(like *zaldiko*, the man-horse), the purifying noise of the cowbells, and ancestral dances.

Many festivities in honour of patron saints are held in towns and cities in late spring and all summer long. Festivals in the capitals attract thousands of people in one long month that starts on 6 July, with the *txupinazo* in Iruñea, and ends in late August when the *Marijaia* goes up in flames in Bilbao. The rest of the month is a succession of events: the Sanfermines, the festivals in Baiona, those of the Virgen Blanca in Gasteiz, and *Aste Nagusia* (Semana Grande or big festive week) in Donostia and Bilbao. The most renowned festivals of all are undoubtedly the Sanfermines, known worldwide for the wonderful atmosphere in the streets and the running of the bulls.

The festivities are not limited to the centre of large cities. They are held everywhere, from the outer suburbs to the most isolated hamlet. They all have a patron saint to honour with religious processions known as *romerías*, followed by a communal lunch in the open air and sports contests. Almost all of them set up the customary *txosnak*, booths that make the functions of a tavern. They are usually staffed by volunteers and the money raised is used to finance the festival or for other social, political or cultural purposes.

Some of the country's most peculiar festivals are the ones held in Lekeitio (with its *Antzar eguna*, a day in a goose game is held in the port); the running of bulls in Falces and Tafalla; the *zikiro-jana* in Zugarramurdi consisting of communal lunches in the mythical caves; , multitudinous pilgrimages to mount Ernio, and celebrations linked with local identity and the recovery of the Basque language, as in the *Baztandarren Biltzarra* in Elizondo.

After summer the farm fairs are held. The most renowned ones for their festive atmosphere and crowds are the October farm fairs in Elizondo and Gernika; the *Euskal Jaiak* in Ordizia with its famous contest of ewe's milk cheeses; the Santa Luzia farm fairs in Urretxu and Zumarraga; and the markets of Santo Tomas in San Sebastian and Bilbao.

Christmas celebrations close the annual season. In recent years a new custom has spread throughout the country: the *Olentzero*, a character that brings gifts to children, whose pagan origin is linked to the celebration of the winter solstice. In most Basque towns and cities, festive parades featuring an Olentzero are held in the afternoon that precedes Christmas Eve. In addition, in some places, it is customary to go from house to house singing carols and raising funds on the very same day of Christmas Eve, San Esteban, and New Year's Eve.

festivals and traditions

Dance with sticks or makil-dantza

The zamaltzain performs a few steps in the maskarada in Soule/Zuberoa.

The giant Miel Oxin surrounded by the txatxoak. Carnival in Lantz (NAFARR

The joaldunak waken nature with the sound of their cowbells between Ituren and Zubieta.

Drums in Donostia on the eve of San Sebastián

festivals
and traditions

Detail of a dantzari

Katximorro, the person who leads dances in the Rioja Alavesa

A very SOCIABLE country

One of the characteristics of the country that surprises travellers to Euskal Herria is its odd and, at the same time, high degree of sociability. It is true that in recent years there is less social activity in the streets, but, even so, Basques like community life. Families are highly important and remain at the core of personal relationships, despite the enormous changes in the past forty years. The family continues to be central to Basque sociability, despite the loss of the extended family nucleated around a hamlet that still persisted in some areas in the 1960s and 70s, and although new types of families have developed in recent years recent years (single parents, divorcees, unmarried partners, or of the same sex).

The next social environment is, normally, the gang of friends. In the past the gangs were segregated into boys and girls, but now they are mixed and share most of the social activities, especially the *poteo* or *txikiteo*, i.e. the rounds of the local bars. The rounds used to consist in drinking wine and singing. Today the musical vein has almost disappeared, and the fuel is much more varied, though beer is generally more popular. The consumptions are paid jointly, with each person contributing to a common fund or paying the cost of a round.

Gastronomic societies, also known as *txokoak*, are an extended version of the gangs of friends. Their members and close friends come together to cook, eat and socialise. The expenditure is based on a system of mutual trust among all the members.

That same trust governs an ancient custom that is still preserved in Euskal Herria. It is community work, known as *auzolan*. In the past it was very common for neighbour to assist each other in tasks that required more labour than an individual family had (manufacturing lime, threshing and husking corn, for instance). They also did community work, like building and maintaining public works, road maintenance, construction or repair of shrines and so forth. Thus, the Basque tradition is mostly community-based individualism.

Several cultures serve as a vehicle for young people to socialise. Pictured, a skater in Deustua (Bizkaia).

An lively atmosphere of drinks and groups of friends in a side-walk café in Bilbao. Below, gaztetxe in Bonberenea (Tolosa).

The auzolan concept, which still exists in small towns, is at the root of many of the initiatives that have defended the Basque identity and culture over the past few years, to the point of becoming a distinguishing characteristic. Anonymous community work launched the first *ikastolas*, the *gau-eskolak* (night schools to teach the Basque language to adults), the recovery of the popular festivals after Franco and as a reaction to government decisions that are considered unfair, like the closure of the newspapers *Egin* and *Egunkaria*. That same tradition inspired the properties self-managed by young people (*gaztetxeak*) that emerged in the 80s in much of the country, despite the evictions. The properties are usually abandoned buildings that the squatters use for a social purpose. In some places they have become referential. One example is the *gaztetxe* in Gasteiz, a busy property in the old town with over thirty years of uninterrupted social and cultural activity.

The *auzolan* spirit was transferred to the business world, at least in part, in the hope of creating a social alternative to capitalist enterprise. This led to the Basque cooperative movement, the most powerful one in the world, around the town of Arrasate, in Gipuzkoa. In the 1950s, the priest Jose Maria Arizmendiarrieta started to organise cooperative workshops in the region of Debagoiena, first in the industrial field (with Fagor as standard-bearer), then in savings banks and insurance (Caja Laboral, Lagun Aro), distribution (Eroski) and higher education (Mondragon Unibertsitatea). Despite the serious setback of Fagor's arrangement with creditors of Fagor at the end of 2013, the Mondragon Group employs more than 80,000 people through 250 companies. Although Mondragon is the huge giant of cooperativism in Euskal Herria, there are, of course, many other companies of social initiative.

But perhaps the Basque willingness to cooperate and socialise is especially observable in the Korrika, a unique fifteen-day popular race held every two years that covers nearly two thousand kilometres on the roads of the seven provinces. This initiative in favour of the Basque language is organised by AEK, a language teaching network for adults. The race travels through the capital, towns, villages, hamlets and lots by day and night, without stopping at any time, while a baton is passed from hand to hand. Sometimes the Korrika are the thousands of people who run along the main avenue of a big city; other times is reduced to a small group of volunteers who cover the vast distances between the towns in La Ribera by night. The baton is crosses the country from hand to hand, without stopping, thanks to a massive, generous and anonymous collective effort.

GASTRONOMY
with stars

It could be said that all the ingredients we have mentioned until now have conspired to forge an outstanding cuisine. Raw material of the highest quality thanks to the wealth of fish in the Gulf of Biscay, the abundance of pastures that has fed the livestock, a mild climate that is suitable for growing vegetables, and a few ports open to world trade and products from the new world. With them, with those vegetables, fish, meats and dairy products, the Basques have developed many traditions in which the gastronomy plays a key role in important celebrations and everyday social events.

Above, delicious beans ladled from the pot. Below, slices of cod cooked in the style of Bizkaia and pil-pil.

Thus, many products of Euskal Herria have attained renown, as well as some gastronomic customs and countless restaurants and chefs. Michelin stars abound in a country where the kitchen has acquired a status and development that aim to be among the best in the world. Euskal Herria boasts several highly prestigious restaurant and catering schools, which were joined in 2011 by the Basque Culinary Center, a university faculty of gastronomy located in Donostia.

Throughout history, numerous products and dishes have attained a high gastronomic level in Euskal Herria. Beans (the ones from Tolosa

Chefs Juan Mari Arzak and Elena Arzak taste a dish in the kitchen of their restaurant.

and Gernika are particularly appreciated), chocolate (from Baiona, Jewish chocolate makers spread it to France), sweet peppers (extraordinary, the ones from Ezpeleta, Gernika and Lodosa), and potatoes (mainly cultivated in Araba) came from America. Vegetable gardens also grow produce of recognized quality, such as the Navarrese peppers and chilli peppers from Ibarra. The main meat has always been beef and lamb, not to mention pork products, including all its delicatessen meats, with unique products such as the Baiona ham, black puddings with vegetables, and the *txistorra* (a sausage made of minced pork). Last but not least, the main fish species are cod, hake, tuna and anchovies.

The most famous dishes of Basque cuisine include *porrusalda* (broth of chopped vegetables with potatoes), *marmitako* (tuna with potatoes), the *ttoro* (a fish soup typical of Donibane Lohizune), the *kokotxak* (hake cheeks), *txipirones* (baby squid) in their own ink, pil-pil style cod, and desserts such as the *gateau basque* (Basque cake) and the *intxaur-saltsa* sauce (walnut sauce).

To all these dishes we must add the creativity and desire to experiment of a new generation of cooks in the 1970s who began to look at other cuisines around the world (especially France) and new trends to expand their culinary repertoire. The main drivers of that current today are chefs of recognized prestige, like Juan Mari Arzak, Pedro Subijana, Ramon Roteta and Hilary Albelaitz, who have been joined by Martin Berasategi, Andoni Luis Aduriz and Eneko Atxa. The list of major Basque chefs is very extensive, and includes such household names as Karlos Arguiñano and Angelita Alfaro. And the source of young chefs is extraordinary.

However, the prestige of Basque cuisine is mainly due to the relatively simple act of eating well. It is so simple that sometimes you don't even have to sit in a restaurant. You just have to follow another Basque tradition, tasting *pintxos* in the local bars. *Pintxos* or *banderillas* are the equivalent, to a certain extent, of what are known as *tapas* in parts of Spain, small portions of food, often arranged on a slice of bread. Originally they were snacks that accompanied the *poteo* (the rounds of bars with a gang of friends) before lunch or

A young lady opens the tap in a barrel of cider. Below, leeks stuffed with salmon, topped with Roquefort sauce.

A well-stocked bar of pintxos in a bar in Donostia.

dinner, but in the last few decades they have developed to the point that is a temptation to have *pintxos* for lunch or dinner, to try out the most exquisite morsels from each bar.

Among the many traditions connected to the gastronomy, the cider houses deserve a mention the cider houses. It is customary to go to them during the cider season (from January to April) to eat the typical menu (cod omelette, cod with peppers, chops and walnuts with cheese and quince) while enjoying the cider as it is poured from the casks. Most of the cider houses are concentrated around Donostia.

Maite ditut
maite
geure bazterrak
lanbroak
izkutatzen dizkidanean
Zer izkutatzen duen
ez didanean ikusten uzten
orduan hasten bainaiz
izkutukoa...
nere baitan pizten diren
bazter miresgarriak
ikusten.

JOXAN ARTZE

I do love
our land
When mist
hides it from me
when it doesn't
let me see
what it is concealing
those outstanding places of beauty
that arise within me

JOXAN ARTZE